# The Price of the Haircut

**ALSO BY BROCK CLARKE**

*The Happiest People in the World*

*Exley*

*An Arsonist's Guide to Writers' Homes in New England*

*Carrying the Torch*

*What We Won't Do*

*The Ordinary White Boy*

# The Price of the Haircut

STORIES BY

## Brock Clarke

ALGONQUIN BOOKS OF CHAPEL HILL   2018

Published by
ALGONQUIN BOOKS OF CHAPEL HILL
Post Office Box 2225
Chapel Hill, North Carolina 27515-2225

a division of
WORKMAN PUBLISHING
225 Varick Street
New York, New York 10014

This is a work of fiction. While, as in all fiction, the literary perceptions
and insights are based on experience, all names, characters, places, and incidents either are
products of the author's imagination or are used fictitiously.

The stories in this collection were previously published as follows:
"The Price of the Haircut," *AGNI*; "The Grand Canyon," *Ecotone*; "What
Is the Cure for Meanness?," *One Story*; "Concerning Lizzie Borden, Her Axe,
My Wife," *The Missouri Review*; "Good Night," *The Sun*; "Our Pointy Boots," *Ecotone* (reprinted in the 2010 *Pushcart Prize: Best of the Small Presses* anthology); "The
Misunderstandings," *The Virginia Quarterly Review*; "That Which We Will Not Give,"
*New England Review*; "Cartoons," *Forklift, Ohio*; "Children Who Divorce," *Ninth Letter*;
"The Pity Palace," *The Virginia Quarterly Review*.

LIBRARY OF CONGRESS CATALOGING-IN-PUBLICATION DATA
Names: Clarke, Brock, author.
Title: The price of the haircut / stories by Brock Clarke.
Description: First edition. | Chapel Hill, North Carolina :
Algonquin Books of Chapel Hill, 2018.
Identifiers: LCCN 2017043775 (print) | LCCN 2017054653 (ebook) |
ISBN 9781616208240 (ebook) | ISBN 9781616208172 (trade pbk.
original : alk. paper)
Subjects: LCSH: Social satire—Fiction. | LCGFT: Short stories.
Classification: LCC PS3603.L37 (ebook) | LCC PS3603.L37 A6 2018 (print) |
DDC 813/.6—dc23
LC record available at https://lccn.loc.gov/2017043775

10 9 8 7 6 5 4 3 2 1
First Edition

For Michael Griffith,
Keith Morris, and
Trent Stewart

# CONTENTS

# The Price of the Haircut

On Monday, an unarmed black teenage boy was shot in the back and killed by a white city policeman. On Tuesday, there was a race riot in our city, a good-sized one. On Wednesday, the mayor formed a committee to discover why there had been a race riot, and on Friday he held a news conference to announce the committee's findings. The mayor told us (we were watching the news conference at David's house, because David's house had the biggest TV and was farthest away from where the riot had been) that the committee had initially believed the race riot had been caused by a white city policeman, who shot in the back and killed an unarmed black teenage boy—because there had been other unarmed black teenage boys shot in the back and killed by white city policemen, fifteen in the last five years to be exact, and because, of course, the riots had happened the day after the boy had been shot—but the mayor put the matter to us as he'd put it to the committee: that this was too familiar, too obvious; that riots had been caused by events like this too many times already; and that would-be rioters would be desensitized, bored, even, by such a thing, and would never, at this late date, riot for such a reason. The mayor had scolded the committee for their highly unimaginative findings, said that they should be ashamed of themselves for falling back on such a tired rationale and for not thinking outside the box (and we were a bit ashamed of ourselves, because we, too, had assumed that the riots had been caused by the shooting, and that meant we were stuck thinking inside the same box as the committee).

Anyway, the mayor told the committee that its initial findings were no good and that they should go back and find something else. And so they did, and this time, the mayor told us, the committee had found the true cause of the riot: it had been caused by a barber named Gene who charged eight dollars for a haircut and who had said something racist while giving one of these eight-dollar haircuts, and the customer who had been getting the eight-dollar haircut had responded in kind and the word had gotten out, and one thing had led to another and to another until it finally led to the riot. The mayor brought out charts and graphs that showed, exactly, how one thing could lead to another, and he also brought out eyewitnesses and experts who testified that, yes, indeed, this barber was to blame for the race riot, and then they showed us an enlarged picture of Gene, who had a good head of white hair and a thick white mustache and large glasses with translucent plastic frames and who looked much like all our grandfathers, which made sense, since each of our grandfathers had also said not-a-few racist things in his time, and all in all the whole presentation was convincing in the extreme. The mayor concluded by saying that he was certain this revelation would help begin the difficult racial healing process and restore our confidence in our unjustly criticized police officers, and then the news conference was over.

"Wow," we said, turning off the television set. "*Eight-dollar* haircuts."

Because for years we'd been paying fifteen, seventeen, sometimes *twenty plus* dollars for haircuts, and the haircuts weren't ever good, weren't ever good enough to justify the amount of money we'd spent on them, and often, after we'd had our hair cut, we'd sit around telling each other that the haircuts didn't look *that* bad, that maybe if we *parted them differently* they would look better, and that in any case the bad haircuts would eventually *grow in*, and it was embarrassing for us, grown men all, to have to sit around and lie like this to ourselves and to each other about our awful, expensive haircuts. It was emasculating, if you thought about it, and we did, all the time: we thought, for instance, about how we could never imagine our fathers sitting around telling lies about *their* haircuts, and how this was another way in which we'd failed to live up to their example, and how if we were to continue to get such bad haircuts, then our self-esteem would be totally and permanently in the crapper and if we were to continue to pay so much money for those bad haircuts, then our sons wouldn't be able to go to the best colleges, either, and would end up like us, graduates of cheap state universities who had unfulfilling jobs and who sat around, fretting about our bad, overpriced haircuts.

Because they really were bad haircuts, and we really had paid way too much for them. Trent had paid fifteen dollars to get a severe Roman centurion haircut that Mark Antony might have been jealous of; Michael had paid seventeen dollars to have his sideburns butchered so badly that one was gone entirely and the other had, somehow, gotten longer, thicker, more muttonchop-ish; David had paid *twenty-five dollars* to get a haircut that was all business in the front, all party in the back. Right after he got that haircut, David ran into his ex-wife on the street (all of our wives had left us, and although they, our now-ex-wives, never said as much, we all knew they had left us in large part because of our bad haircuts, and who could blame them, really: because who would want to be with a man with such an awful haircut, and who could respect a man who paid so much, time and time again, for such an awful haircut?), and she took one look at him and said, "Hey, nice haircut."

"Really?" David said.

"No," she said.

"She actually said that," David told us. "And then she laughed; it was a mean laugh." David was wearing a baseball cap when he told us this story—he was, like the rest of us, over forty and too old to wear a baseball cap—but none of us called him on it, because of his truly horrific haircut and what his wife had said about it, and, believe me, our empathy for him was huge, especially mine: because I can't even tell you how bad my haircut was and how much I had paid for it. Even now, it's too difficult to talk about.

But maybe it wouldn't hurt so much to have such bad haircuts—we'd resigned ourselves to having bad haircuts; we'd known no other kind—if we didn't have to pay so much for them. If we only had to pay eight dollars for our haircuts, then it wouldn't be nearly as awful, nearly as humiliating. It would have been like we were getting a *deal* on our bad haircuts. That was our thinking.

"But wait," Trent said. "What about the riots? Are we really going to give this racist barber our business?"

He had a point, and we spent a highly engaged few minutes discussing the matter. Because the riots really were horrible and life-changing for so many people—so many abandoned and not-quite-abandoned buildings set on fire; so many white motorists pulled out of cars and beaten; so many department stores ransacked and looted; so many black men harassed, beaten, shot at with rubber bullets, maced, and arrested by police in riot gear. So many restaurateurs and nightclub owners who had risked all by investing in the impoverished but architecturally significant part of town where the riot had taken place; so many of these brave pioneers who had gutted and refurbished these architecturally significant buildings and

who had turned them into brewpubs and sushi bars tricked
out with Italian marble and complicated track lighting, who
had made a successful go of it and had managed to convince,
with their many off-duty police officers as security, white sub-
urbanites that it was safe to come back into the city again, at
least for a few hours on a Friday or Saturday night—these
people were ruined, too, or at least their investments were,
or at least their investments were until the city came through
with the no-interest loans it was promising to these restaurant
and nightclub pioneers. Yes, the riot really had been horrible,
and were we, as right-minded, left-leaning, forward-thinking
men of the world, were we really going to patronize the hate-
ful barbershop that had caused all this misery and destruction
in our city?

Because we really were right-minded, left-leaning, forward-
thinking men of the world. For instance, the day after the riot
we had all leapt into action. David, who teaches history at one
of the underperforming city high schools, sent his ninth grad-
ers to the school resource center to watch videos of civil distur-
bances from throughout our nation's history. Trent, who works
at the main branch of the city library, scrambled to set up a
display of books by Malcolm X, Larry Neal, Maya Angelou,
and other radical black writers, even though it wasn't anywhere
near African American History Month. Michael, who's a waiter
at a local steak house, began soliciting and accepting dona-
tions from his customers on behalf of the dead black teenager's
mother and father. Me, I work in a silk-screening shop, and we

had all these T-shirts left over from the last riot—twelve or so years ago now—that read NO JUSTICE, NO PEACE, and I put them in boxes outside the shop, with a sign on the boxes that said the T-shirts were free to any socially conscious citizen who wanted them. But was all this enough? Wasn't it also our duty to do something proactive and civic-minded in the wake of the riots, like not get our haircuts, no matter how cheap they were, at the racist barber who had caused the riot, as the mayor had so clearly demonstrated?

But as David argued, that was easy for the *mayor* to say: because he had an excellent haircut, and no doubt he had an excellent haircut because he had the money to pay for it, and because it was easier to get an excellent haircut after already having had previous excellent haircuts, and you could only get those previous excellent haircuts if you had the money to get them in the first place. And then there were the four of us, who could not afford and had never been able to afford the kind of haircut the mayor had, who were permanently shut off from the world of excellent hair by virtue of our middling salaries and our long history of bad haircuts, and yet we were also doomed to pay too much for these bad haircuts, much like the black people who rioted were doomed to pay too much, for instance, for lousy foodstuffs at the understocked and over-priced neighborhood grocery store, the only grocery store they could go to, because it was the only one within walking distance and so few of the residents of the neighborhood could afford cars. Because when you thought about it, David said, we were helpless, just like the rioters were helpless; we were caught in a vicious cycle, just like the rioters were caught in a vicious cycle; we were desperate, just like the rioters were desperate, and desperate people do desperate things, things they probably shouldn't. Yes, desperation made the rioters riot, and desperation would make us get eight-dollar haircuts at the racist barber, too.

Well, it was a spectacular piece of logic all right, and we sat there quietly for a while, as if the logic were something beautiful in the room, something so very beautiful that it was the exact antithesis of our so very ugly haircuts. We sat there awhile, admiring the logic, contemplating it, not wanting to disturb it, until David, who owned the logic and had the right to decide how long we would sit there in silence admiring it, finally broke that silence and said, "Come on, let's go."

We went. Went to get our haircuts at the eight-dollar racist barber who was responsible for the riot that had torn apart our city. But we didn't go with a collectively light heart; don't think that we did. No, rest assured that we were a very grave bunch as we piled into Trent's station wagon and drove over to Gene's to get our haircuts. We were somber all right, full of the enormity of what we were doing, the significance, the complexity, and in some way, we felt more human than we ever had before: because if, as someone once said, to be human is to be compromised, then we were feeling very human indeed. Because there was the half of us that wanted our cheap haircuts, that felt we deserved them, were owed them by someone—*society* maybe—but the other half of us knew that what we were doing was very wrong, and that we'd have to do something to make it a little less wrong, a little more forgivable, something that might enable us to explain away and justify our actions later on. Not that we had second thoughts about getting our cheap haircuts (we didn't, and would not be deterred), but we all agreed that something had to be done to make it known that we were not just garden-variety bigots getting our hair cut for eight dollars at the racist barber. We needed to assure people—ourselves, too—that we were against what we were doing even as we were doing it. Trent, who is the most politically active of our group and who has spearheaded many a protest in our city and who owns his own bullhorn and who even, at that very moment, had generically worded protest placards in his car, suggested that, after we had actually gotten our haircuts, we should picket the barbershop to express our outrage, etc. It was an interesting idea all right, except that it might leave us a little too exposed as hypocrites, and we didn't want that any more than we wanted to pay exorbitant prices for our bad haircuts. Michael, who, as mentioned, waits tables and is very much concerned with gratuities, suggested that we shouldn't leave the barber a tip, but this didn't seem a big enough gesture, especially since we never tipped any of our barbers and certainly had no intention of tipping this one. Finally, we decided to do the very least we could do: we would keep our ears open and our eyes peeled, so that we could explain later on how very awful it was at the racist barber, how we'd had no idea how severe the problem was and how horribly racist the barber actually was, but now we could easily understand how he had caused the riot, and now that we knew, we had no intention of ever, ever letting him cut our hair again, even if the haircut was incredibly cheap, only eight dollars, which was something of a miracle, if you considered it in the context of all the other pricier, albeit not racist, barbers.

There was a big crowd milling around outside the barbershop when we pulled up. This was not unexpected. In fact, in the car we had discussed what we would say to the big crowd milling around outside the barbershop. We assumed that the crowd would be there to express their outrage at their barber and how he was responsible for the riot that had rocked our city, and we also assumed the crowd would largely be black, and since they were largely black they wouldn't be able, right off, to understand the difference between us and the regular patrons of the barbershop, might even mistake us for the bigots who had caused the riot, etc. But that was far from the case, as we would make clear. Because even though the barbershop's neighborhood was largely white, none of us lived in that neighborhood; the white people who lived in that neighborhood were called "Appalachian." At least Trent, whose ex-wife worked for the city census bureau, said that was what they were called, officially, and this was what we called them in public and around people we didn't know very well. When we were talking among ourselves, we called them white trash, and we would explain to the black protestors that we were as scared and distrustful of the people in the neighborhood as they were, and, aside from the color of our skin, we were as different from the regular patrons of the barbershop as they, the black protestors, were. And what if the black protestors then asked, as they no doubt would, why then, if we were so different from the bigots who normally frequented the barbershop, were we going to get our haircuts there? It was a good question, and we would admit this to them, right before we would hand over the figurative microphone to David, who would then put forth his theory about the vicious cycle of our bad, overpriced haircuts, and how this made us much like the rioters and maybe the protestors, too, who probably had their own variation on that vicious cycle, that vicious cycle which made us close kin, brothers, really, and as brothers, couldn't they cut us a little slack? This would work; we were certain of it. Because, of course, the black protestors would be able to see our haircuts, which were, as you know, incredibly bad.

There were two problems with this plan. One, the protestors outside the barbershop weren't black; they were white. We found this troubling in the extreme. Where were they, the black people of our city? Had they had not watched and listened to the mayor's televised press conference? Had they not heard the committee's findings? Had they not scrutinized the very convincing charts and graphs? Had they not taken to heart the testimony of the experts and eyewitnesses? Had they not seen the picture of Gene? Did they not care that this racist barbershop was the cause of the riot that had rocked our city?

Were the black people of our city this politically apathetic? Were they content to leave their civic and political and social well-being in the hands of these white protestors? Yes, it was a blow to all of us, because David's theory had been so convincing and we had all begun to feel a special kinship with these black people, had begun to feel that their race and our hair were like an enormous door, and on one side of the door were the questions and on the other, the answers—the answers that had always been kept from us. But maybe, we thought, we could open the door together. Except the black protestors we'd expected weren't here. Did they not want to open the door? It was mysterious all right, and we didn't pretend to understand it, just as we didn't pretend to understand why getting overcharged for awful haircuts made men like us so very unhappy.

Speaking of men like us, that was the second problem with the white protestors: they weren't protestors. We realized this after we'd piled out of Trent's station wagon and gotten closer to the throng. These people had no signs or placards, were holding no megaphones or chanting any chants. No, they weren't even a throng. They were merely waiting in line, quietly, to get into the barbershop. They were customers, would-be customers, and more than that, they weren't the Appalachians from whom we were prepared to distinguish ourselves. No, they were middle-class white men wearing moderately expensive running sneakers and white ankle socks and khaki shorts and polo shirts, just like us, and just like us, they all had very, very bad haircuts.

Well, we had no idea, no idea how epidemic this problem was, no idea that there were so many men just like us, and it stunned us to be in such a large community of man. It made us mighty uncomfortable, to be true, and for several minutes we stood off a bit from the line, as if the line had nothing to do with us. Because we had for years thought ourselves as antagonistic to the larger community, whatever that larger community might be. Our haircuts had made us outsiders, rebels, if you will, which was the only good thing we could ever think to say about them. And so you can understand why we didn't get in line right away. But that seemed silly, after a while: because we so obviously belonged in the line; our haircuts told everyone that we belonged in that line, and in this way our haircuts betrayed us *again*. And so we gave in and did apparently what one does when one finds oneself in a community of man: we got in line with the rest of the community and waited to get our cheap haircuts.

It was a very *tense* wait. At first, no one spoke. At first, we all stared straight ahead at the badly cut back of the man's head in front of us. Then, after a few minutes, David asked, meekly, if anyone knew anything about Gene. Someone said that he'd heard he had been a prison barber, that he was a white supremacist with Aryan tattoos. This was dismissed right away as mere rumor. Someone said that he, Gene, was continually aphoristic, and sometimes the aphorisms were racist and sometimes they weren't. This fit in with our earlier impression of Gene as grandfatherly, and we were quiet again for a while as we thought again about our grandfathers, and our mixed feelings about them, too, and then Michael said something vague and generic about the riots, how he understood why the riots had happened and how he didn't blame the rioters one bit. It was difficult to disagree with this, and we didn't, and everyone murmured their assent, until Trent wondered out loud where all the black people were, wondered why they weren't protesting and picketing the barbershop, chanting angry slogans, that kind of thing. All of us in line agreed that we found this absence somewhat curious. And then someone piped up and said he'd heard that there were large crowds of black people at the police headquarters downtown, picketing and protesting the white cops' shooting of yet another black teenage boy in the back. This got everyone in a bit of a lather. Because hadn't these protestors listened to the mayor's news conference and the committee's findings? And were they, too, guilty of not thinking outside the box? It seemed like they *were* guilty of this, and now that we thought about it, the riot itself hadn't exactly been innovative, either. Because what earlier had seemed impressive, so momentous and important and life-changing, now seemed obvious and tired, with all the same old looted grocery stores and white people pulled from cars and beaten, etc. Now that we thought about it, we were ashamed of the riot, too, as it was pretty much the same old, same old. "That riot was a *disgrace*," I said. "What were those black rioters *thinking*?"

I didn't stop there, either: no, I went on and gave voice to what had always disturbed us about the black people in our city, those black people who had rioted and who were now down at the police headquarters for absolutely no good reason; who never seemed to appreciate our right-minded, left-leaning, forward-thinking (albeit sometimes theoretical and moral as opposed to active) support of their struggle against oppression and who never responded to our friendly "yos" and "what ups" when we greeted them on the street; who never seemed to appreciate how uncomfortable these greetings made us, who never seemed to understand how fraudulent we felt saying "yo" and "what up," but that we suffered it because we wanted them, the black people of our city, to know that we were on their side, rhetorically speaking, that we were willing to meet them on their linguistic turf. But they never seemed to appreciate the gesture, never responded in kind; or, if they responded at all, it was with glares, awful, withering glares, which made us wonder if there were something *wrong* with these black people, if they really knew who was on their side and who wasn't and if they really wanted our help, if they wanted help at all, and for that matter if they even wanted to help themselves. And then there were their haircuts—the hair extensions and the high fades and the cornrows and the old-school pick-in-the-hair Afros—these haircuts that were so very expensive and yet, we thought, so very ugly, and yet they got these haircuts *on purpose*, unlike us, who had no choice, these people made a conscious decision to pay too much for their ugly haircuts, and not only that: they didn't call them haircuts.

Oh, no, one didn't cut hair, one cut *heads*, which we found more than a little barbaric and which made us wonder—again, again—what was *wrong* with these black people, these black people who were now, with their intentionally expensive and hideous cut heads, protesting down at the police headquarters when they knew very well that the riots had nothing to do with the police and had everything to do with Gene, and so I spoke for all of us when I asked, at the top of my lungs, "What is *wrong* with these black people?"

I immediately suspected that I'd said something inappropriate, because everyone started shuffling their feet nervously and even David, Michael, and Trent wouldn't meet my eyes. I thought about apologizing for what I had said, was about to point out my haircut and how truly horrific it was and how it often made me say and do things I shouldn't. It made me, for instance, often speak for the four us, for the collective *we*, instead of for myself alone: because it somehow seemed less lonely to speak for four men with bad, overpriced haircuts than just one; because it seemed less lonely to be four men against the world instead of just one. At first, we all liked it, me saying "we" instead of "I," but then the more we thought about it, the more pathetic a coping device it was, and we all agreed that it was odd and awful that the thing that is supposed to make you less lonely ends up making you more so. And we also all agreed that I should stop referring to us as *we* and start referring to the distinct individuals we were. And I tried—we all knew I tried—but often I failed, often I slipped up and still spoke for the group, and I blamed that on my awful, overpriced haircut, too.

But it turns out that I didn't have to make excuses this time, because a man with an extraordinarily wide side part said, "It kind of makes you angry, the whole thing," and then someone with a greasy, uneven brush cut went one step further and said he knew what it was like to get angrier and angrier until there was nothing to do with the anger but let it out. There was a more vocal assent to this, and a couple of men in line, men with the worst of the worst haircuts, gave each other high fives. One man who had large trapezoidal bare patches on the back of his head wondered out loud why the line wasn't moving. "Has anyone gone into the barbershop, or come out?" he wanted to know. One person had gone in, it turned out, but hadn't come out yet. So had anyone seen Gene's work? No one had, and this made things even more tense. "What happens if his haircuts are worse than the ones we already have?" one man with nasty-looking razor cuts on his neck asked. "What happens if the mayor got it wrong, if the haircuts are more than eight dollars?" another man wanted to know. "They had fucking *better not* be more than eight dollars." The man who said this smacked his meaty right hand into his left palm, and it was like a call to arms, and the whole line suddenly took up this call to arms and said we could not take it anymore, we had been pushed too far and, all of sudden, we were on the verge of our own riot. Because you can't push people around for too long; you can't treat them like second-class citizens forever. You can't expect them to just sit by and take it. You can't. You can't.

Then the door opened. Everyone got quiet, profoundly quiet, and then a cheer went up. Because we could see the guy who'd had his hair cut, and it wasn't bad, not bad at all! It wasn't perfect—there were stray hairs peeking out on the sides, and his receding hairline had been slightly accentuated instead of obscured—but all in all, it wasn't a terrible haircut, and it gave us great hope: you could almost feel the crowd elevate a little, rise up at the sight of his haircut and in anticipation of the next question—not "Did Gene say anything racist?" but "Did it only cost you eight dollars?"

"It did," the man said. "It really did! I gave him a ten, and I left him a dollar tip, and I still have a dollar left over!" Here, he waved the dollar bill at us, over his head, like his and our own little flag.

And would you believe the world changed a little bit right then? It became a little brighter, a little more hopeful, and all of us in line changed a little bit, too, became a little brighter, a little more hopeful, and a little more generous, a little more empathetic. We would be better, happier people from there on out; we were all certain of it. We even felt more generous toward the black protestors, no matter how deeply buried they were in denial and self-deception and self-destruction. After all, who were we to judge? We were where we needed to be, and maybe *they* needed to be down at the police headquarters, and maybe at that very moment they, too, were massed in front of a door, waiting for their old bad helpless lives to die and their new selves to be born. Maybe, like us, they were watching that door swing open for the first time; maybe, like us, they were waiting patiently in line to cross that threshold, so happy to finally leave the question and enter the answer.

# The Grand Canyon

My husband and I went to the Grand Canyon on our honeymoon, I don't know why, it wasn't close-by, neither of us liked the desert, or hiking, or canyons, it was as though we had made a deal with someone, our parents, God, some other only-somewhat-interested third party, that we would be allowed to get married only if this somewhat-interested third party were allowed to choose where we would go on our honeymoon, so anyway, here we were, at the Grand Canyon, making the best of it, I guess, and speaking of making the best of it, in high school I was good at painting, my art teacher had said so, he'd said, hey, you're good at painting, you should take some art classes in college, and I'd always wanted to do that, take art classes in college, but my major, which was elementary education, didn't give me enough time for that, which was fine, I loved teaching the kids, or at least I loved the idea of teaching the kids, but I also loved the idea of being a painter, the thing that my major, my chosen profession, had not allowed me to be, and as it turned out the Grand Canyon was very popular with painters, they were lined up easel-to-easel at the rim, the South Rim, the North Rim was too far away to see clearly, but presumably they were lined up there, too, but the painters were definitely out in full force at the South Rim, I couldn't believe how many of them there were, I mean, you expect hikers at the Grand Canyon, backpackers, mule riders, rafters, just regular tourists who aren't after anything in particular, and, yes, even honeymooners, I guess, but I never expected it to be so popular with painters, so popular that a kind of small industry had grown up there around them, and you could rent an easel and a canvas and a palette and a brush, and while they didn't rent stools for you to sit on while you were painting, I had brought my own stool, a collapsible camping stool, and thinking of it now, that's probably why we went on our honeymoon at the Grand Canyon, not because some somewhat interested third party had chosen it for us, but because you could camp there, which was of course much cheaper than staying in a nice hotel somewhere, but then it was also the Grand Canyon, and so it wasn't as depressing going there for your honeymoon as it would have been if, say, you'd camped in Gravel Creek State Park in Donville, Ohio, which was the state park in our hometown and we had never camped there, but if we had camped there on our honeymoon it would have been much more depressing than camping at the Grand Canyon on our honeymoon, I guess, so anyway I'd brought my camping stool, which my husband had, along with all our camping gear, purchased at a steep discount at the sporting goods store, because he worked at the sporting goods store, but regardless, I'd brought the collapsible camping stool to sit on during my honeymoon at the Grand Canyon, and now I brought it even closer to the Grand Canyon, right up to the South Rim, and I remember, it was the third day of our honeymoon, our third day of five days, and where was my husband at that moment when I was about to start painting, I didn't know, I supposed he was jerking off somewhere, because that's what he'd threatened to do less than an hour before, when I told him I didn't want to have sex, because we had had sex several times on the two previous days and nights, and because we'd had sex many times leading up to our honeymoon, because after all we had lived together for three years before we were married, and we had sex many times during those three years, and also during the two years of dating before that, and, wait, there was another reason I hadn't wanted to have sex with my husband less than an hour before I had decided to follow my long-lost passion for painting, but what was the reason, oh yeah, I remember, it was because we were in a fucking tent, we had been having sex in a fucking tent for two days and I just didn't want to have sex in a tent again, not for the third day, and when my husband asked what about days four and five and I said, "Probably not then, either," and my husband said, "Fine, I'll go jerk off somewhere," which wasn't really much of a threat, I mean go ahead and do

that if that's what you want, it's all right by me, although come
to think of it I hadn't seen my husband since that moment,
less than an hour earlier, when he had charged right out of the
tent, and it's not like I was going to wait around for him, no,
so not long after he'd left, I'd picked up my camping stool and
brought it to the South Rim and rented all my painting stuff
and only now did I wonder where my husband had gone to,
where he was, and if he was jerking off there, and if he was
jerking off right into the Grand Canyon, and if so, and even
if not, wow, I thought, I'd love to paint a painting of him
doing that, but I wondered how difficult it would be, to get it
exactly right, to do justice to the image of my husband jerking
off into the Grand Canyon, because back in high school I was
good with landscapes, I was very good painting landscapes,
but I was not so good with the human form, and I wasn't good
with scale, either, and I thought how depressing it would be to
have this fantastic image to paint, this image of my husband
jerking off into the Grand Canyon, and not being able to do
it justice, of making the figure of my husband jerking off into
the canyon so small that you couldn't see him or so big that he
was as big, or bigger, than the canyon itself, yes, I could see it
now, he would be a giant, I would screw up and make him into
a giant, because I was so terrible at scale, and also so terrible
at drawing the human form, and so I'd end up with a giant
stick figure stroking his giant stick penis on the rim of a tiny
Grand Canyon, and that's not even taking the ejaculate into
consideration, although I supposed I wouldn't have to paint

the ejaculate, the painting could be of any moment during the jerk-off but before ejaculation, which was a shame, because I thought I could at least paint ejaculate and have it be realistic, if I was even going to go for realism, and was I even going to go for realism, I hadn't decided, maybe I would go for surrealism, and if I was going for surrealism, then maybe the giant stick figure of my husband, etc., would be appropriate, whereas if I was going for realism I probably wouldn't be painting the giant stick figure of my husband or his ejaculate, no, if I was going for realism, then I would probably end up painting a painting of a tent next to the Grand Canyon, and in that tent would be my husband, sulking, not having jerked off anywhere, wondering where in the general Grand Canyon National Park I was, when I was coming back, would I have sex with him when I did, and I knew if I painted that realistic portrait I might end up getting divorced and if I ended up painting the other one, well, I might end up staying married, and which was better, marriage or divorce, I didn't know, just like I didn't know which was better, realism or surrealism, and while I was sitting there wondering all this, the woman (we were all women at the South Rim) sitting next to me on her own camping stool behind her own easel asked what I was thinking, and I told her, and when I was done telling her, she nodded empathetically, like she knew exactly what I was going through, and said, "You know, maybe you should start small, like just painting the canyon, and then see where things go from there," and so that's what I did.

# What Is the Cure for Meanness?

The first gift that died was the lilac bush. I gave it to my mother after Dad had left her and moved in with Julie from work. Because Mom was pretty depressed—not just about my father leaving her, but the *way* he'd left her, on her birthday, her fifty-second birthday, with the cake right there on the table, the vanilla cake with vanilla icing and blue HAPPY BIRTHDAY! lettering and pink flowers, the cake that my mother had made for herself, as always, the cake that my dad said was so crummy, even though he hadn't eaten any of it yet, because, he said, he didn't even have to eat any of this *particular* cake to know it was crummy, because the birthday cakes she had made over the years were *always* crummy, because my mother couldn't bake her way out of a paper bag and how could she not know, at this late date, that she couldn't bake her way out of a paper bag? After all, hadn't he told her so? Hadn't he told her many, many times that she couldn't bake her way out of a paper bag, and hadn't he also mentioned how she had let herself go over the years, that her arms were too skinny and her belly strangely big and protruding for someone with such skinny arms, and then there was her hair, which was too brittle and dry from the way she bleached it—which he had always insisted upon, because he liked her (liked her better? disliked her less?) as a blonde; he was a big enough man to admit that he had insisted upon her bleaching her hair and so the blame was partially his and he could shoulder it; but now her hair felt like straw, and could he be blamed for wanting to be with a woman whose hair felt like hair (Julie's hair felt like hair, I assumed) and not like hay? And he didn't like Mom's personality much, either, and while he was on the subject, did she have to be such a life-killing, humorless hag who hadn't even laughed when he called her birthday cake crummy? ("Get it?" he asked. "Cake? Crumbs? Crummy?") All in all, Dad said, it was totally understandable that he, Dad, was leaving her for Julie, never to return, and for that matter, it had been kind of *noble* for him to have hung in there for as long as he had, and he hoped that she would think hard about how noble he had been before bad-mouthing him to any of their friends, assuming any of their friends would, now that he was leaving Mom for Julie, choose to be friends with *her* and not *him*. Which he highly doubted.

With that, my father got up from the table, left the room, and went upstairs. My mother and I sat there, breathing hard, as if my father had taken most of the oxygen with him. My mother's expression was so blank it couldn't really be called an expression. Neither of us said a word, but I was thinking two things—*My poor Mom*, and *Will he take me with him?*—when my father came down a few minutes later, suitcase in hand, and my mother asked, "Did you ever love me?"

"And you ask too many stupid questions," my father said. "That's another thing."

Then he left. We sat there for a while longer. I was staring at my mother, who was staring at her birthday cake. I was sixteen years old, the time in your life when you make your big irreversible choices, and I knew right then that my big irreversible choice was this: Was I going to be like my father or mother? Was I going to be a mean, bullying son of a bitch, or was I going to be kind and gentle and selfless and *good*? Was I going to mistake power for happiness, meanness for pleasure? Was I going to be the kind of person who made himself feel good by making the people he was supposed to love feel bad? Or would I be the kind of person who would, for instance, work hard to turn a loving mother's worst birthday ever into something not so awful, not so devastating? My father was out there somewhere with Julie and her hair that felt like hair; but I was here, with my mother, on her birthday, and my father hadn't taken me with him: he had made his choice, and now I was going to make mine. And speaking of my choice, I had a personal essay due for Mrs. Tooley's English class the next morning, and up until that moment I had no idea what it was going to be about, other than it was going to be an essay

about something personal; but now that I'd made my choice
to be like my mother and not my father, I at least had the title,
which was: "I've Made My Choice (I Am My Mother's Son")."
And as my first official act as my mother's son, I picked up a
knife and said to my mother, "OK, birthday girl. Who's ready
for some cake?"

"I am," my mother said feebly. But before I could cut her a
piece, she started flapping her hands in front of her face, the
way she always did when she was upset, like her sadness was
a smell she could get rid of by flapping her hands spastically,
like a retard (which was the way Dad always described it), the
hand flapping and her, the hand flapper. "I'm sorry, Bryan,"
she said, and she jumped up from the table, ran up the stairs,
and locked herself in the bathroom. After a few minutes, I
knocked on the door and asked her what she was doing, and
she said she was holding one of Dad's razor blades at that very
moment and was seriously contemplating slicing her wrists
with it, which I doubted, since Dad used an electric shaver
and had most likely taken it with him, in any case. But still, I
felt pretty bad.

When I went to school the next morning, my mother
hadn't killed herself (she was asleep, not dead, and I knew she
wasn't dead because she was snoring, snoring that weird high-
pitched, siren-like snore that was loud enough to be heard
through her closed door and my closed door, too, and Dad
once woke Mom up to say that the neighbors had been com-
plaining about the noise and suggested she sleep on her back,

or her side, or maybe in a different neighborhood altogether, and he also said her snoring had caused the neighbors to give her a nickname: The Following Is a Test of the Emergency Broadcast System. This Is Only a Test), but I still didn't know how to make her feel better, and I hadn't written my personal essay, either. So when it was my turn to get up in front of the class and read what I hadn't written, I instead recited my title, told the class basically what I've told you, then turned to Mrs. Tooley. She was looking at me the way you might look at someone with a horrible, disfiguring illness: part *You poor thing* and part *Are you contagious?*

"Your poor mother," she said.

"Tell me about it," I said. "What should I do?"

"You could start by being nice to her."

"Already done that," I said. "But what else? Should I get her something?"

"Get her something?" Mrs. Tooley said. "You mean, like flowers?"

"Hey, that's a good idea," I said. So after school, I went out and got my mom a lilac bush. And I didn't get her just any old lilac bush. It was a *Korean* lilac, because the people at the nursery said that the Korean lilac symbolized hope, grace, and rebirth, whereas the American lilac didn't symbolize much of anything and was just your normal flowering bush, basically. I brought it to back the house, planted it right in the backyard garden (which, like my mother herself, had gone to seed, and was scraggly and barely presentable—this is what I *thought,* but I didn't *say* it, unlike my father, who would have, and in fact had, so many times), and told my mother what it symbolized and that, no matter what Dad had said, she was a good person and a great mother with a lot of excellent qualities and a full life ahead of her. And that I loved her.

"Oh, sweetie," she said. "Is this my birthday present?"

"Birthday present," I repeated, not quite getting it.

"I thought you'd forgotten to get me something," she said. "I had started to think that maybe you'd forgotten to get me something for my birthday."

Because I had forgotten to get her something for her birthday, which had been, as you know, the day before. I'd forgotten to get my mother a birthday present. This was indefensible, and I didn't try to defend myself. But if I *had* tried to defend myself, I would have said something about school and trying to get and keep my grades above a D, like my mother was always bugging me about, and not having time to remember to get a birthday present for each and every person on this planet and how, besides, I'd remembered most of her other birthdays and my track record wasn't all that awful, if you thought about it, and Jesus, I was *here*, wasn't I? Unlike another person who had also failed to get her a birthday present, I was at least *here*. Although if she kept giving me this sort of guilt trip, maybe I wouldn't be much longer: maybe I'd go out and find a different mother, the way Dad had gone out and found a different woman. And then there was the Korean lilac bush. Hadn't I gone out and bought this highly symbolic lilac bush just to make her feel better? Hadn't I gotten my hands and my favorite jeans all dirty while putting in it the ground? Did she know that I was being selfless and doing this all for her? Did it matter whether I gave her the bush on her birthday or the day after? Did it matter whether I'd gotten it for her birthday or just to make her feel better, regardless of the day and out of the goodness of my heart? Didn't my mother know how hard she was making it, already, for my heart to be good? Didn't my mother know how hard she was making it for me to be like her, and not Dad? These were just some of the things I could have said in my defense but didn't. Instead, I said, "I'm sorry I didn't give this to you yesterday." And then: "Happy birthday, Mom."

"Oh, Bryan, I love it. But will you take care of it for me?" she asked. "Because you know I'm not too good at taking care of plants."

"I know," I said. Over the years, my mother had killed all variety of houseplants, in all variety of ways, and there wasn't one green, living thing in our house except for the mold in the back of the refrigerator. Speaking of the mold, just a week earlier my father had said that if the mold got any bigger and more disgusting and animate, then it would end up eating her, my mom, its creator, and then someone would make a horror movie about it, and my dad and I laughed: because he was funny— my father could say some funny things even when he was being such a huge bastard—you had to give him that.

"So you'll take care of the Korean lilac for me?"

"I said I would, didn't I?" And then, hearing my father's

voice in my own—not the funny father's voice, but the one who didn't have enough patience with the way my mom needed to be reassured about every little thing. It was *that* father's voice that I heard, not the funny one at all, and so I said, more gently, in my own voice: "Yes. I'll take good care of it for you."

"Thank you," my mother said. She leaned over, smelled the purple flowers, and smiled at me. "This is the nicest birthday gift anyone has ever given me."

And then it died. I woke up two weeks later on a Saturday, went down to get some breakfast and juice, and there was my mother, coffee cup in hand, staring at the Korean lilac, smack in the middle of the garden, brown-leaved and cobwebbed and so dead it would have won a deadest plant contest, hands down. *Huh*, I thought, and then: *Oh well.* Because after all, the Korean lilac had lasted two weeks, which was probably a long time for such an exotic bush. It'd had a good run. Besides, the bush, when it was still alive, had really seemed to cheer Mom up: she was locking herself in the bathroom less often and had started washing her hair with this special conditioner to make it less hay-like. Of course, the Korean lilac wasn't *magic* or anything; it couldn't work *miracles*, and the first time Dad had come by the house, to get some clothes he'd left behind, Mom had reverted to her old pathetic self and begged him to stay, and had even held him by the ankles to prevent him from leaving, and he'd dragged her across the floor until finally shaking her loose (and I felt for my father a little bit: because Mom really made him look undignified and like a caveman, the way he was dragging her across the floor like that; she'd put him in an impossible position, really, even though he dragged her as gently as possible, didn't kick at her at all or scream, "Get your hands off of me, woman," like he easily could have done, but instead said, quietly, patiently, when he got to the front door, "Are you going to let go of me now, or am I going to have to drag you down the steps and out onto the sidewalk?" I was grateful for his tact and would have told him so, except that he didn't even seem to notice that I was there, holding the door open for him). But by the third or fourth time, my mother just let my father take whatever he wanted—furniture, flat- or stemware, even stuff that was my mom's from before they were married—and I attributed this sea change to the Korean lilac. Yes, she had gotten some of her dignity back, thanks to the Korean lilac, and, hell, I had, too: during those two weeks I'd spent only two days in after-school detention, I'd hit only one kid in the back of the head standing in line in the cafeteria (he was moving so slowly and asking for it, and even then I restrained myself and could have hit him much harder, and with more knuckle), and I even tried to pay attention in my classes, even did my homework, or some of it. Because, I figured, education might be the cure for meanness, and if I had my father's mean gene, I thought I could maybe learn it out of me. This was what I was trying to express to my English class in my Alternative Forms of Poetry presentation, during which I got up, grabbed a book off one of my classmates' desk, and rapped, "What, what, what is the cure for meanness?" and then pointed at the book and rapped, "This, this, this is the cure for meanness," which would have come off a lot better if the book hadn't been a driver's ed manual and if I hadn't been holding it upside down. The class started laughing at me—even Mrs. Tooley was smiling and shaking her head in an amused way—and I almost told her and them to go fuck themselves. But I didn't; that's the point: I didn't tell my teacher and classmates to go fuck themselves, and I had the Korean lilac to thank for that, and my mother did, too, and we couldn't really ask more of it, I didn't think.

But then I looked over at my mother and she was crying, crying the way she tends to: silently but open-mouthed, the tears running down her cheeks and into her mouth, as if she were her own irrigation system. Or maybe she was her own drainage system. If I'd paid more attention in my earth science class I ended up failing, I would have known which one.

"My Korean lilac bush died," my mother said during a pause in her quiet weeping, and then turned and looked at me meaningfully, *as if it were my fault.*

"Hey, don't blame it on me," I said. "It just died on its own. These things happen."

"I'm not blaming you," she said. "But is it possible you didn't water it enough?"

"Oh, I watered it," I said. Because I had; twice, thrice, sometimes four times a day I'd watered that bush, giving it a serious soaking each time. "I definitely watered it."

"Maybe you watered it too much," she said.

"Let's not argue about how much I did or did not water the bush," I said. "I can get you another one."

"I don't want another one," my mother said. She started crying again, and there was so much liquid going in her mouth that I thought she might drown—drown from drinking her own tears—and how awkward that would be for me to try to explain it to the investigating authorities, and how hard my life would be afterward, when it became known that I was the son who let his mother drown in her own tears. So I felt bad again and begged her to stop crying. "Please," I told her. "Please. I'll get you anything you want," and I listed all the things she might want: a tree (a birch maybe, because my mother had grown up in Massachusetts and was pretty nostalgic about birch trees and what that poet wrote about them and what the Indians did with them), or maybe a fern, or a bonsai, or one of those very pretty flowering miniature trees whose fruit or blossoms or leaves were deadly if eaten or touched for an overlong time, or sometimes even just sniffed. But, no, my mother said she didn't want any of those things: all she wanted was her family back, and no plant or tree or bush was a family, and besides, those things were like everything else and would only, like the Korean lilac I'd given her, end up leaving her, betraying her, and making her feel even more lonely and like dying herself. "I don't want another plant," she said, and then she ran upstairs and locked herself in the bathroom before I could point out that it wasn't a "plant"; it was a "bush," and you would have thought at her advanced age, she'd have been smart enough to know the difference.

But in any case, I got the message—*plant life* of any kind was out—and so I got my mother a dog. This time, I was smart and didn't do anything too fancy, like look for a heavily symbolic exotic-but-not-so-hearty dog. No, I did the smart thing and I went right to the pound, right to the good old-fashioned all-American pound, and looked for the most weathered pooch they had, a dog that had seen the worst the world had to offer and had survived, and was still around and barking and eager to provide a lonely discouraged middle-aged woman a little canine companionship. After a little searching, I found one: way in the back of the pound, in the cage closest to the incinerator, I found a ravaged but sweet-tempered one-eared 110-pound pit bull who had so much spark in him that he nearly chewed his way through the cage while I was standing there, looking at him, trying to picture him in our house, in the backyard, curled up in front of the ventless gas fireplace, thinking about what kind of companion he'd be to my mother. The way that dog kept lunging at me, it was like he was making a case for himself: it was like he was saying, *Me! Me! Please pick me!* I asked the guy in charge how much the dog cost, and he said, "Man, you can just *have* him," and he handed me Jugular's (that was the dog's name) choke collar and chain from his dogfighting days. They were the strongest, thickest choke collar and chain I had ever seen, and must have cost someone a pretty penny; but the guy offered to give them to me gratis, just like the dog, which was pretty much the clincher as far as I was concerned. Besides, I thought Mom might appreciate my frugality, because we were on a pretty tight budget since Dad had left us and neither Mom nor I had a job, nor were we qualified for one, at least not any decent-paying ones, and I figured that if we really got desperate, then Jugular probably had a few more dogfights in him and maybe we could make some money off of that. Which was another plus.

Anyway, I brought Jugular home and presented him to my mother. As a token of my love for her. In giving my mother Jugular, I was actually saying: *I am your son, and this is my heart, and I am giving it to you.* Although at first, she didn't take it that way. At first, she was dismayed by the way Jugular pulled on his chain and frothed at the mouth and gnashed his teeth when she reached out, tentatively, to pet him. It was the gnashing of teeth in particular that concerned her.

"Will he chew on things?" my mother wanted to know.

"He's a dog," I said, through gritted teeth, because I was trying to hold Jugular back from my mother and he kept lunging at her, and it seemed like the only thing standing between my mother and a mauling was the choke chain and my arms, which were kind of spindly, which was something I'd gotten from my mother: I'd gotten her skinny arms and not my dad's biceps, which really were impressive and which sometimes, while watching TV, he rubbed, as if giving them a good shine. I repeated, "He's a *dog*, Mom. Odds are he'll probably chew on something."

"Maybe he'd like to chew on my slippers," my mother said. She took off her slippers, her slippers my father had gotten cheap at the factory outlet store—there was something barely wrong with them, some weak seam or irregular stitching or substandard lining—and had given to her for her *last* birthday, and put the slippers under Jugular's nose and let him sniff them, first the left and then the right. Jugular stopped pulling on the chain immediately and started wagging his little stump of a tail. He took the left slipper into his mouth gently, as though the slipper were a duck he didn't want to wound, and hopped up on the couch next to my mother, where he sat, contentedly chewing the slipper my father had given her, just last year.

"Thank you, Bryan," my mother said, petting Jugular, who looked up at her fondly while still gnawing on the slipper. "It was a very thoughtful gift. You're a wonderful son. I'm so lucky to have you."

"OK," I said, not really listening to what my mother had said. Because I was thinking about the dog chewing on the slipper that my father had given my mom just last year. He'd given it to her *just last year*; that's one of the things that bothered me. Was this the way my mother treated her gifts? Was this the way she would treat Jugular in a year? Would Jugular end up in the mouth, so to speak, of next year's gift? After all, my dad had probably spent a lot of time rummaging through the slipper bin and picking out those slippers, and here they were, just a year later, in a dog's mouth, and no wonder no one gave my mother birthday presents. Did she ever think about that? And then there was the dog on the couch. On the couch! Where I wasn't even allowed to put my feet, a plate of food, a glass of milk! Was this to say that I was less important than Jugular? That I was less important to my mother than a dog she had just met? It made me never want to give my mother a gift again, and I nearly strung that choke collar around Jugular's neck and dragged him back to the pound, where fate would deal with him a lot sooner than next year's present would.

But, no, I wouldn't do that. My mother looked so happy, sitting there on the couch with her dog, so happy and so grateful and so close to contentment. So I swallowed my many legitimate grievances, or tried to, and when I was trying to, I had this very thought: Who knew it would be so difficult to be good? Who knew that the people you're trying to treat well would make it so difficult on you? Who knew that supposedly good people could tempt you into meanness, could actually force meanness upon you? Who knew that you could watch your mother, on the couch with her dog, so happy that she was *glowing*, the way she never glowed when she was sitting there on the couch with her husband or, for that matter, her son, as if the dog were a better companion than her own flesh and blood? Who knew that you would have to ignore your mother's lack of simple human consideration and that it would be such a struggle just to be happy for her, to be able to give her such happiness and expect nothing back in return? But I didn't expect anything in return, I didn't, and was truly happy for my mother, even when Jugular finished with the left slipper, spit out its remains right on the couch, and started in on the other slipper.

Because that's what the dog did for the next week: he ate slippers, on the couch, with my mother sitting next to him, saying, "That a boy, Jugular. Good boy." Luckily, that's what my father had always given to my mother for her birthday when he remembered it—slippers—and so my mother had plenty of them to spare. But it's not like she had an infinite supply of slippers, and one night she finally ran out. It was a night when, as it happened, my mother had gone out to dinner and a movie with a few of her "lady friends" (and I was happy for her, that she was finally feeling good enough to get out of the house and have a little fun; it was a positive development for her, and I was pleased to have played such a crucial role in bringing it about with my thoughtful gifts. But why "lady friends"? Did anyone even use the expression "lady friends" anymore? Had anyone really ever used it at all? I actually asked my mother these questions (because I'd written two poems—"I Gave My Mother My Heart and She Fed It to the Dog, Which I Had Also Given Her" and "It Is Difficult to Be Good"—for extra credit for Mrs. Tooley's class, and after she'd read them, Mrs. Tooley told me that it was ingenious the way I challenged the conventions of rhyme and meter by not using rhyme and meter at all, and then she gave me a little lecture about how I was right, that it's easy to be mean, and hard to be good, but that nothing good ever came out of meanness, and that I needed to be nice to my mother, nice to everyone, of course, but especially to my mother. And speaking of my mother, Mrs. Tooley suggested that my mother and I talk more often and more honestly about our problems, so that our life together would get better and maybe my poems about our life together would get better, too), and my mother said, "Fine, 'girls' night out' then." When she said this, I snorted and, before I could stop myself, said "*Girls*, ha!" My mother stared at me, ashen-faced, as if seeing an unwelcome ghost. I knew whose ghost it was, and so I recovered somewhat and said, "Have a good time!" But Mom kept staring at me and staring at me, until finally she said, "Just take good care of Jugular. OK, Bryan?").

And that's the point: I would have taken good care of Jugular, except we ran out of slippers. He spit out the remains of the last one in the house not ten minutes after my mother had left for her *girls'* night out, and so we had a little problem. Because that dog and I were like two guys who got along better when they were in the company of women (or *ladies*, or *girls*), and now that Mom was gone, we just sat there on opposite ends of the couch. After a while, I began hearing low growls coming from Jugular, from somewhere deep inside him and rising up through his jowls, his teeth, and I kept saying, "There are no more slippers. Do you understand, you idiot dog?" But whether Jugular understood or not, the growls kept coming, and I didn't know what to do.

So I called my dad. He hadn't given me his and Julie's home number, but I had his work number down at Kahn's, where he was the night foreman. I called the number and made my way past and through a series of female secretarial voices (I thought one of them might have been Julie's: it was a happy, high voice, and it filled me up with this longing, the kind of longing that sometimes made me do things that got me in trouble at school, like scrawl flattering obscenities on Tracy Carpenter's locker, to name one of many; her voice made me want to say "You might know me: I'm Bryan Reid," and have her say, "Oh, Bryan, your father talks about you all the time, and your voice, it sounds so much like his, except kinder, more full of goodness") until I finally got to my father. I knew it was my father because, upon answering the phone, he said, not "Hello," but "What?"

"Dad," I said. "It's me, Bryan."

Which started my dad swearing—at me, I thought at first, but then some of the swearing was punctuated by instructions about casings and packaging, and I realized he was talking to some of the guys on the line, who were fucking up, apparently, and at least *I* wasn't and that was something in my favor—and then my father came back to me and again said, "What?" I told him about the dog, and his slippers, how they were all gone, and then I paused, thinking that maybe this would rile him up: that he would throw down his rubber gloves and whip off his protective mask and come home and avenge his slippers, and maybe stay home to ensure that no further harm came to whatever else he might have given us, or what he might yet give, and maybe in the bargain save me from trying and failing to be good and like my mother all the time—because I knew now it was easier to seem like a good person when my father was around, with him so obviously not being one. Plus, I missed him: for those reasons and for a bunch of others I didn't exactly understand, I missed him and wished he would come home. But my father didn't say anything when I told him about the sorry fate of the slippers, and so I went on and told him about the dog *right now*, his growling, his drooling, his teeth, and then I paused again. Still, my father said nothing, and so I was forced to be direct: "So what do I do, Dad?"

"What?" my father said. "*That's* why you called me *at work?*"

"Yes."

"At *fucking work?*"

"Jugular's a big dog, Dad. Mean, too. I'm a little scared," I said. "Please."

"Think, Bryan," my father said, and I almost expected him to reach through the receiver and tap my forehead, hard, with his forefinger, like he used to do during happier times when we were in the same room and he wanted me to think. "Aren't there any other shoes in that house?" Then he hung up.

"Thank you," I said to the dial tone. I hung up the phone, told Jugular to stay, got off the couch, went upstairs, gathered all the shoes in the house—all the sneakers, work boots, dress pumps, loafers, deck shoes, baseball cleats, flip-flops, and the golf spikes my father had left behind, even the old hockey skates that I'd grown out of—and threw them in a pile on the couch, in the place where I'd been sitting. "Go ahead," I told Jugular. "Chew." Then I went upstairs to work for a few minutes on my English homework (Mrs. Tooley was making us write a short story, and mine was very short, and it was about this man, this mean bastard, who was a mean bastard not because it was *easier* to be a mean bastard than it was to be whatever its opposite was but because being a mean bastard gave him a certain *critical distance*, a *perspective* from which he could find the solutions to all the most difficult problems, and for that reason he also lived in a cave deep in the woods, where he waited for his only son to find him and assume his birthright, which had something to do with being a problem-solving mean bastard who lived in a cave) before I fell asleep at my desk, only to be awakened four hours later by my mother's screaming.

Because the dog died, too. It must have been the golf spikes, or maybe the baseball cleats, or possibly even the hockey skates. Something sharp, that was clear. Whatever it was, by the time I got downstairs, Jugular was dead, and there was blood everywhere—on Jugular, obviously, and also on Mom from her hugging his corpse, and all over the couch, too, which was pretty much ruined from the dog's blood, which was poetic justice if you ask me. Although my mother didn't ask me: she was too busy screaming, screaming about poor Jugular and how everything she cared about up and left, or died on her, and that she was doomed to be what she was now: alone, all alone, for the rest of her life.

*"All alone?"* I asked—yelled, even, to be heard over my mother's wailing. Because, OK, my mom was upset, what with the dog dying a bloody death so soon after the Korean lilac shriveled up, and dying so soon after my father left her on her birthday. But was I not there, standing right there in front of her, in the same house, next to same bloody dog and couch? Was she saying that being with her son, her only son, was exactly like being all alone? "Are you saying that being with me is like being all alone?"

After I said this, my mother closed her eyes and shook her head, then opened her eyes again. "I can't believe it," she said, sucking back a tear. "You sound exactly like your father."

"The hell I do," I said. And then: "But you know what? Maybe Dad was right to leave you. I bet Julie doesn't take him for granted like this."

This was probably the wrong thing to say, because it made Mom hold Jugular closer and start wailing again, even louder than before, certainly loud enough for our neighbors to hear. If she kept crying this loudly, sooner or later the neighbors would come over to see what was wrong, and there my mother would be, with the dead dog and blood all over both of them, and me standing over them, with my fists clenched (my fists were clenched) and that I'm-so-mad-I-might-kill-someone look on my face (I knew that look well enough from my father's face, could feel it settling onto my own face, and, sure enough, I went to the mirror and there it was), and I knew that I had to do something, and so I said, "I have school tomorrow. I'm going to bed."

My mother didn't answer me, didn't look at me, either; she kept holding the dog, rocking back and forth, whimpering until she got tired of whimpering, wailing until she got tired of wailing, but not paying attention to me no matter what sorry sound she was making.

So I went to bed. It wasn't exactly a restful sleep—in part because of Mom's crying and, later, a loud, protracted thumping, which I assumed was Mom dragging Jugular's lifeless body across the living room and then the kitchen, and then outside to the backyard, where she would bury him; but also because I was thinking, wondering how I'd gone so wrong with Jugular. That's what I asked Mrs. Tooley the next day, after she'd read my short story and kept me after class, because it was so very short and apparently wasn't really a story, either, and so I was going to have to rewrite it, and I asked her, "How did I go so wrong with Jugular?"

"Who?" Mrs. Tooley asked. "What?" She looked at my story, as though maybe Jugular was a character in it she'd forgotten. So I told her: about the dog and the slippers and my father's advice and the shoes I'd fed him and how he died chewing on them and about my mother wailing and saying she was all alone and that I sounded like my father, and then me saying my father was right to leave her for Julie, and whatnot.

"Wait a minute," Mrs. Tooley said. "*You* got mad at your *mother?*"

"Sure," I said. "For saying she was all alone." Mrs. Tooley looked over her glasses at me, as if she didn't understand what I was saying, and so I clarified: "She wasn't alone. I was right next to her."

"Bryan," she said, in that kind, patient tone teachers use when they're preparing to stop being so kind and patient. "You fed that poor dog ice skates. You fed him golf spikes and baseball cleats."

"He liked to chew on shoes," I said. "That was his thing."

"You *killed* your mother's dog and then blamed her for feeling lonely," Mrs. Tooley said, then slid my very short story across her desk toward me. "And then you wrote a story praising your father who left you and your mother, and who suggested you feed the dog the skates in the first place."

"He never said 'skates' per se . . . " I said, but Mrs. Tooley put up her hand to stop me.

"You know what I think?" Mrs. Tooley asked, and then, before I could say whether or not I wanted to know, she said, "I think your mother is right. I think you probably sound just like your father."

"I don't," I said.

"I bet you do," Mrs. Tooley said. She took her pencil out of the crook of her ear and jabbed it in my direction. "Do you *want* to sound like your father?"

"That's the thing," I said. "I don't know how not to," and

then I started crying: because it's a terrible thing, not to know how not to do something you know you shouldn't do. It's worse than not being able to conjugate a verb, to solve for pi, to memorize all the symbols for all the elements in all their tables. "I don't know how to sound like my mother, and I don't know how *not* to sound like my father."

"Why don't you try to sound like yourself?" Mrs. Tooley asked, her voice kind again (because, as the standardized tests would have us put it, a student's crying is to a teacher as water softener is to water). She put her pencil back above her ear and handed me her teacher's box of tissues, which I took. "Why don't you use your own voice?" she suggested.

"My own voice?" I asked, still sniffling. "What's that?"

Mrs. Tooley opened her mouth to answer, but then the bell rang and the classroom started filling up with students from Mrs. Tooley's advanced class: the tide of smart kids came in, and I was washed out, into the hall, with Mrs. Tooley's box of tissues and the advice she'd given me. *Why don't you use your own voice?* This was good advice, no doubt, and like most good advice not entirely useful. How could I find my own voice? How does one do that? Wouldn't it be easier to find another person, someone who wasn't either my father or mother, and use his voice? That seemed like a more reasonable plan. And since I knew my mother felt *all alone*, and since I missed my dad, I decided I would find a new man for her, and a father figure for myself, and then make my voice sound like his.

Notice, I said *new* man; notice I said father *figure*. Because I knew that neither of us wanted my actual father, from whom I was trying to distinguish myself and by whom my mother had been persecuted for so many years and was to trying to forget, and in the same way trying to remember what it was like to be loved and appreciated and to feel like a real human being again. No, the trick was to get a man who was the opposite of my father. My father's name was Richard, and his nickname was Dick. So I thought that maybe I'd start off by finding a man whose name or nickname was the opposite of Dick.

The thing about such a quest is this: it's time-consuming, and so I had to take a week or so off from school while I looked for this guy. I looked at the public golf course, the downtown mall that no one ever went to, the afternoon movies at the arty movie theater near the university, and the coffee shops in the same neighborhood. I kept coming up to strange men more or less the same age as my mother, coming up to them singly and in groups and asking, "What's your name?" and then "What's your nickname?" And what did I discover? I discovered that there are lots of strange men, who, if you come up to them and ask these questions, will ignore you or tell you to bug off, and I also discovered, from the men who *did* answer my questions, that the world is full of men with dull, depressing nicknames, like Spook, Stutz, Link, and Shoe. It took me ten whole days until I found someone good, in the IGA, scrutinizing the bratwurst selection: a man who was maybe a young sixty. He was wearing an Irish-looking wax jacket and a red scarf and penny loafers, and had healthy red cheeks and a good head of white hair, and I came up to him and asked, out of the blue (this was my method), "Hey, what's your name?"

It's odd what will or will not get someone's attention. When I asked him this question, he didn't turn around to answer; he simply said, "Champion," and kept pawing the sausages. But when I asked him, "What's your nickname?" he actually turned to face me.

"My nickname?"

"Yes," I said. "What do people *call* you?"

"People call me Champ," he said, and then he smiled at me, as though he knew he'd given me the right answer.

"That's perfect," I said. "Come with me."

He came. Because it turns out Champ was a widower, a new one, and he was as eager for companionship as Mom was, as I was, although soon he would regret being so eager, and this is one of the things I've learned: there are plenty of sad and lonely people in the world, and if you're unlucky enough to be one of them, then sooner or later someone even lonelier and sadder will find you and bring you home with them, and then you'll regret it.

But anyway, Champ was a great guy. At first, I was worried, because he looked classy, classier than we were (it was the penny loafers that made me think this), and when I first pulled up to the house, I was seeing it as he was seeing it: with its dirty aluminum siding and its unmowed front lawn (Jugular had left his mark) and our faded green plastic porch furniture. I thought Champ would say something snide about the house or make a sour face and I'd have to punch him, unexpectedly, in the back of the neck, the way Dad had taught me to with people who were bigger than me. But Champ didn't; he said, "What a nice home," like he meant it. So I brought him inside. Luckily, by now, my mother had cleaned up Jugular's mess; there were even new slipcovers on the couch, and my mother had cleaned herself up, too, somewhat, but she still looked tired, beaten down, and older than she was. I felt ashamed, for her, for me, and wished I were with the dog, somewhere in the backyard where no one could get to me; for the first time, I understood completely the saying "Lucky dog." My mother must have felt ashamed, too, because she said, "I'm sorry I'm such a mess. My dog just died."

"That's terrible," Champ said. He had a way of saying nice things like he meant them, and when he said, "That's terrible," about the dog dying, you knew he meant it, whereas if my father had said, "That's terrible," you knew he wouldn't have meant it at all. Although he probably wouldn't have even said, "That's terrible"; he probably would have said, "That's what dogs do," or, "Get over it." But not Champ; he said, "That's ter-rible," and then, "I'm so sorry," and then, "My name is Champ."

Oh, you should have seen my mother's face when Champ told her his name! You could see time divide in two for her: in the past, there was a man named Dick, and in the present, there was a man named Champ. In the past, there was a man who wouldn't take her anywhere (except to the emergency room that one time when she fell off the roof while replacing the shingles Dad refused to replace himself, because he had put them up in the first place and had done his part already), and in the present, there was a man who would take her dancing at the club (Champ really did belong to one) every Saturday. In the past, there was a man who, when Mom and Dad were in public, walked a step ahead or behind her, because she was either walking too damn fast or too fucking slow; in the present, she had a man who would let her put her arm through his, who would *stroll* with her, who wasn't at all ashamed to be with her in public, who would make her happy, who would finally treat her right.

Treat her right, that is, until he died. It was my fault, mostly my fault; I'll admit it this time. Because—and unlike the Korean lilac and Jugular—old Champ didn't even make it two weeks; he didn't even make it through the night. But he did make it through dinner, and I blame part of it on that: the dinner. Because it was heavy, beef something or other, with a sauce that tasted like mushrooms frozen and then melted in whipped cream—and even though Champ said it was delicious, said he'd never had a better beef something or other in his life, in truth it was heavy: you could sort of feel your heart drop anchor after eating it. Yes, it was my mother's beef something or other that did old Champ in, and not the roughhousing.

Because that's what I wanted to do after dinner: roughhouse. I'd always wanted to roughhouse on the floor with a father, or father figure, but my real dad had never wanted to do it, because he said it would hurt his knees to get down on the floor and it was degrading and undignified. Plus, the one time he had started to do it, when I was five, he had spilled his beer all over the somewhat new Berber carpet and then he let loose with a string of "motherfucker" this and "cocksucker" that. All this was directed downward, to the floor, where I was, next to the beer stain, and it wasn't clear to me whether my father was swearing at me or the stain until he said, "Jesus, Bryan, go get a motherfucking paper towel and clean that cocksucking mess up, will you?" and then I knew. That was the end of rough-housing on the floor for me and Dad. Or Dick.

But here was Champ. It was after dinner, and he was sitting next to my mother, on the couch. He was my mother's Champ, but he was also mine, was he not? Had I not found him? Did I not have a legitimate claim to him, to his attention? Did I not have a right to ask him, after dinner, after my mom's murderous, heart-choking dinner, "Champ, will you roughhouse with me?"

"Roughhouse?" Champ asked.

"On the floor?" I asked.

Champ looked confused at first, but then I got down on the floor in a wrestling position (freestyle, which they'd taught us in gym class) and he understood and said, in his great, sincere way, "I'd be honored."

My mother was saying, "Oh, Champ, you shouldn't do that. You don't have to do that," but Champ did it anyway: he took off his penny loafers, handed my mother his cardigan, and got down on the floor. And we roughhoused.

And then he died, too, right there on the Berber carpet (it was the same carpet my father had spilled beer on eleven years earlier) in my scissors lock, which wasn't even that tight. It wasn't even that tight. After all, Champ was old, and his heart and arteries were full of that heavy beef something or other Mom had made, and I'm pretty sure the scissors lock wouldn't have killed him if he hadn't just eaten what he'd eaten. But I didn't want to say this, didn't want to blame my mother for Champ's death, which was clearly what my father would have done. I didn't want to sound like him, didn't want to use his voice. No, I wanted to use Champ's voice and then call it my own. But what would Champ have said to my mother about his own death? It was hard to tell, especially since I'd only known the guy for about five hours. I didn't want to say something Champ wouldn't have said, didn't want to use the wrong voice and then be stuck with it as my own. So I sat there awhile, mulling it over, trying to think of what to say to my mother. Luckily, she didn't seem to be in a hurry to hear anything. After it was clear that Champ had died, my mother had called 911; then she returned to the couch, where she sat next to me, legs crossed, with a calm look on her face as she absently stroked Champ's cardigan, until I finally thought of just the right thing to say.

"Champ was a great guy," I said.

"Yes, he was," she said. "And then you killed him."

"Hey, hold on," I said. "What about that beef something or other you made him eat?"

"Shut up, Bryan," she said. This stunned me a little, since I'd never heard my mother use that phrase, never heard her say anything harsher than a gentle "Hush." I looked at her, waiting for her to apologize, but she didn't. "What are *you* fucking looking at?" she said.

"Wow," I said. "You sound just like Dad."

"Good," she said, and then she said a few more things, too, but I wasn't really listening to them. Because I was thinking how Mom had stopped sounding like herself and started sounding like Dad, too. What did this mean? Did this mean that she wasn't using her real voice anymore, or that this was her real voice all along and was just waiting for her to find it? Did this mean that Mrs. Tooley was wrong? Did this mean that there was no such thing as a real voice? Or did this mean that your real voice was the mean voice you wished you didn't have, and not the good voice you wished you did? Did this mean that there was no cure for meanness? Did this mean that the only problem with meanness was that it made you look for an impossible and unnecessary cure for it in the first place? Was there anything really wrong with taking some pleasure in a little meanness now and then? After all, my mother really seemed to be enjoying herself, now that she had finally stopped trying to be good: she was all smiles as she pointed out how I had killed Jugular and the Korean lilac, asking how could I plausibly pretend I hadn't, and how I was too stupid to live, or maybe I was too stupid to love; I couldn't tell because of how fast she was talking, maybe making up for all the time she'd lost *not* being mean. But she seemed happy, for the first time ever, that's the point, and who was I to tell her she shouldn't be happy, just because the happiness was born out of a little meanness? Who was Mrs. Tooley? Who was anyone?

There was a knock on the door; I assumed it was the police or the paramedics, and so I got up to answer it. But when I unlocked and opened the door, I discovered it wasn't the police or the paramedics: it was my father, his suitcase in hand. He'd obviously just shaven, and his big blue jaw glowed like neon in the porch light.

"Dad!" I said. "Are you coming back to us?"

"Julie kicked me out," he said, and then held up his suitcase as evidence. "She said I was too mean to her. She said she didn't like the way I talked to her."

"She didn't like your real voice," I said.

"Who the Christ knows," he said. "But yeah, I guess I'm coming back."

"But why did you knock on the door?" I asked. "Why didn't you just let yourself in with your key?"

My father leaned over, raised his hand, extended his right index finger. I recognized the gesture, knew that my father was going to tap my forehead, hard, and tell me to "think." I closed my eyes, waiting to be tapped and told. But before my father did so, he must have glanced over my shoulder, must have seen Champ's corpse on the Berber carpet.

"What the . . . ?" he started.

But my mother interrupted. "Bryan, who the hell is that?"

I opened my eyes and called out, "I have a surprise for you," then grabbed my father by his tapping hand and pulled him into the house, into the living room, where my mother sat on the couch, calmly stroking Champ's sweater as if it were a cat. When she saw my father, my mother smiled; it was a huge, genuine, grateful smile, a smile she'd probably been waiting to smile her entire life.

"Hello, Dick," she said to my father, who didn't say anything back. There was a look on his face I'd never seen before: it might have been love, and he might not have expected it—in the plays Mrs. Tooley made us read, love always found people when they least expected it, and whether they wanted it to or not—because he started backing up, toward the front door. But my mother was too fast for him: she sat up, dropped Champ's cardigan, and grabbed Dad's hand, pulled him back on the couch next to her, and sat there, stroking his hand the way she'd stroked Champ's sweater moments earlier. They were both looking at me, as though they were expecting something. Who knew what they were seeing? But as for me, I was seeing a family; finally, finally, I was seeing people who belonged together. I wish Mrs. Tooley had been there to see it: something good could come out of meanness! Who would have thought it possible? And maybe my mother was thinking the same thing, because she said, "Thank you, Bryan. This is the best gift you've ever given me."

"What kind of idiot thing is that to say?" my father wanted to know, but I knew. I knew exactly what my mother was talking about.

"You're welcome," I said.

"Why don't you come sit on the couch next to your father," she said.

"I think I will," I said, and then sat down next to my father, on the couch where Jugular and Champ had once sat, the place where my mother's gifts eventually came to rest.

# Concerning Lizzie Borden, Her Axe, My Wife

On Friday, my wife, Catrine, kicked me out of the house, and on the following Thursday, she called me at my room in the Budget Inn and said, "I want you to come with me to the Lizzie Borden Bed and Breakfast in Fall River, Massachusetts."

I knew this about Lizzie Borden: that long ago she'd made a famous bloody, murderous mess of her parents with an axe and gotten away with it—but before I could ask why Catrine wanted to go to the site of such an awful, violent crime, with me, her estranged husband, she said, "You're not allowed to ask me why I want to go there with you," and so instead I asked, "Will we stay the night?"

"Plus, take the official two-hour tour," she said. Which is how we end up, two days later, sitting in the parlor at the Lizzie Borden Bed and Breakfast and waiting for the official two-hour tour to begin. There are five other people also staying the night, etc.: a married couple from Ohio the color and consistency of cookie dough; a chain-smoking white-haired woman from Long Island, who has stepped outside to smoke twice in ten minutes and who has already purchased and donned the official Lizzie Borden Bed and Breakfast pocket T-shirt with a drawing of the bloodstained axe on the pocket; and two backward-baseball-hat-wearing fraternity boys down from UMass, whose fraternity brothers have told them—as a prank, I'm guessing, as everyone in the room must be guessing, except for the two fraternity boys themselves—that this is the *Lezzie* Borden House—Lezzie Borden being, it turns out, a lesbian adult film star whose childhood home, I suppose, the frat boys think they're in. There is some confusion over this, because the chain-smoker has just advanced the theory that the real Lizzie Borden was also a lesbian, and would have been much happier had she lived in another time, in another place, with another stepmother and father who she wouldn't have had to axe-murder if she'd been allowed to embrace her true sexual self. This business about axe-murdering has thrown the frat boys considerably, and one of them—the thin Laurel to the fatter one's Hardy—keeps rotating his baseball hat back to front to back in disbelief.

"Lezzie Borden killed her mom and dad?" he asks.

"*Lizzie* Borden," says the woman from Long Island, and from the way she says this, through gritted teeth—and from the rainbow cigarette lighter she's fiddling with—I'm guessing she herself is a lesbian. But the boys take no notice of her, and it's easy to imagine them in their introductory English classes, using "me" instead of "I," or "who" instead of "whom," and being corrected by their professors and not paying attention to *them*, either.

"Lezzie Borden killed her mom and dad with an *axe?*" the fat one says. "Because she was a *lezzie?*"

"In *real life?*" the thin one asks. "Or are we talking about . . . ?" and then begins to describe the plot of some movie, at the beginning of which Lezzie Borden has been imprisoned for some unexplained capital crime and who, with her volup-tuous cellmates and prison guards and even a visiting order of reform-minded nuns, is sentenced to spend ninety minutes engaged in some, as the boys put it, in unison, "hot, hot, hot girl-on-girl action." After they've said this, the boys give each other high fives, except that they give the high fives backward, with the backs of their hands instead of their palms, possibly to be consistent with their hats. The chain-smoker stands up and seems on the verge of backhanding the boys *and* their back-ward baseball hats across the room, and the boys—who I'm sure have no idea why the chain-smoker hates them but, like your basic mammals, innately recognize antagonism and how to react to it—puff out their chests like fighting cocks, and into the middle of this potential brawl walks the tour guide, a bird-faced middle-aged woman with her plaid skirt pulled up to midsternum, who takes what is obviously her place, in the very center of the room, between the boys and the chain-smoker, and asks if we've been getting to know each other.

The chain-smoker flicks her lighter and glares at the boys, and now the boys are regarding her warily, as if she might possibly try and set them on fire and they're not sure if their too-long shorts, their flip-flops, their fraternity T-shirts, and their hats are fully fire-retardant, and the Ohio couple hasn't said a word yet except to say that they're from Ohio, and this might be the only thing they're capable of saying, the only thing worth knowing about them, and just then I notice that Catrine is no longer at my side, is no longer even in the parlor, and the silence in the room is huge and embarrassing, and it seems like someone has to say something. So I say: "We were just discussing Lizzie's sexual orientation."

The tour guide smooths out her skirt at this and says, "Concerning Lizzie's sexual orientation, there is no proof of it, whatever it was, nor that it, whatever it was, had anything to do with horrific axe murders, one of which took place in this very parlor and which Lizzie may or may not have perpetrated. We do know, however, that she spent the last ten years of her life with the New York showgirl Molly Sheehan . . ." As she goes on and describes the shows in which Ms. Sheehan appeared and the common assumptions about showgirls in that day and age, the frat boys drift away from the tour guide and over to the pictures of Lizzie on the wall. Catrine and I looked at the pictures when we first walked into the parlor, fifteen minutes earlier, and so I know what the boys are seeing: a severe and not-very-attractive woman in a high lacy Victorian collar, to whom the words "hot, hot, hot girl-on-girl action" could not possibly apply—not now, not a hundred-odd years earlier, when the pictures were actually taken. When the boys turn around, you can see them focus on the house itself for the first time. The house has nothing red or plush or velvet, nothing that screams sex, lesbian or otherwise; I'm seeing it as the boys are seeing it, and it looks not like the home of a porn star but the home their grandmothers might have been raised in, and the people in the same room with them look not like fellow *adult film* devotees but only garden-variety *adults*. And the boys are also no doubt remembering the many other times they've been duped by their fraternity brothers—who, come to think of it, do not share their passion for Lezzie Borden *or* lesbian porn—and I would feel sorry for the boys if I weren't so busy feeling sorry for myself. The pathetic, helpless expressions on their faces ask, *Where are we?* and *How did we get here?* and *Why?* and *Why?* and I want to walk over and give them a backward high five and tell them I know exactly how they feel, that I have exactly the same questions and a big need to have them answered and a big fear that they won't be.

A MONTH BEFORE the Lizzie Borden Bed and Breakfast, Catrine suddenly couldn't breathe the way her history of breathing suggested she ought to. Climbing the stairs was like ascending Everest; taking the garbage to the curb was like an aging and out-of-shape Atlas struggling to hoist this boulder we live on. Small acts of exertion—toothbrushing, shoelace-tying, dog-walking—made her face turn blue, the

way a face as beautiful as my wife's should not. Catrine is not
an athlete—she swings a tennis racket the way she flails away
at bees, and, as a point of comparison, she is terrified of bees,
completely, and so the flailing is considerable and spastic—but
she isn't a bit out of shape, either, and often at night I long-
ingly dream of her lovely, vaguely muscled legs as if they were
distant, unattainable things, even though those legs are right
there in the same bed, sleeping next to me, and if it's one of
the thirty-seven warm, dry days we have per year in Rochester,
where Catrine and I live; then you know she'll be out on her
bike, working up a sheen of sweat on her upper lip, using the
proper hand signals for the proper turns, drenched in sun-
screen and never without her helmet. My wife takes care of
herself is the point, and when she woke up one morning gasp-
ing like a scuba diver without her tank, we knew something
was up. So Catrine took the day off from Mercy High—where
for a decade now she's taught French and English to those
ninth- and tenth-grade girls in their knee socks and plaid
kilts—and went to the doctor. I work for Kodak, as fewer and
fewer of us do these days, and I was in the office, trying to
concentrate on how Fuji does it and how we might do it better,
when Catrine called.

   "Well?" I said.

   "I've got a hole," she said, breathing hard and trying not to.
"In my heart." More audible breathing, and then she started to
cry—big, ragged, heavy sobs, like a tragic Darth Vader weeping into his ventilator. "A big one."

I forgot all about Fuji and the plausible upper limits of high-speed film and drove right home, where I found Catrine sitting on the couch, watching one of the smart, bighearted single-mother-and-daughter-going-it-alone comedy dramas she can't ever not look at. I rushed right to her side and held her hand, which is what you naturally do with sickly people, I guess, and she let me hold it. But it was strange: Catrine's face wasn't blue; her breathing was even and normal, the way it hadn't been for a week. She didn't look like someone with a big hole in her heart, didn't act like it, either, and when I asked her to tell me what the doctor said, she wouldn't tell me until her show was over. So I sat beside her and didn't watch the television and loved the things about Catrine that I always have and still do: the way she makes a soft, gentle humming sound right before she laughs; the way she'll suddenly and violently recline on the couch and fling her legs over mine, as if she couldn't bear *not* to do so any longer. I loved these things until after the credits rolled, when Catrine turned to me and said that she had a congenital heart defect. She said this calmly, with notable disinterest, as if telling me she'd eaten fried ravioli for lunch in the Mercy High cafeteria again.

"What does that mean?"

"Like I told you on the phone. I have a big hole in my heart," she said. "It's probably going to get bigger."

This is what happens when you hear the words "big," "hole," and "heart" applied to your wife, your true and only love: you think immediately of the corresponding hole in your own heart, about it getting bigger and bigger and never closing, and how you will eventually want to die from it but can't and won't. But I didn't tell Catrine this—because as mentioned, she's an English teacher, with strong opinions about metaphors and the way we abuse them, and she would not have been impressed by the way the literal hole in her heart was giving me a figurative hole in mine. Instead, I asked, trying to be positive, "OK. What can we do about it?" which is one of things Kodak teaches us to ask when we've run out of better, more intelligent questions.

"*We* can use this," Catrine said, and held up an inhaler. "No more blue face. No more breathing problems."

"Will it make the hole in your heart smaller?"

"Nope," she said, and before I could continue the line of inquiry, she said, "It's nothing, Eric. Forget about it."

This I did not do. Instead, I went out and purchased a *Merck Manual of Medical Information* and learned that Catrine had now what she'd always had—the hole had been there from birth, small and harmless at first, and had grown bigger and bigger, and you couldn't close it, and she would eventually die from it, and it was impossible for the *Merck* to tell when, but it probably would be sooner and not later. When I read this, the world divided in two: between the life I had lived up until now with Catrine, and the life to come, without her, the life I couldn't imagine and didn't want. And so I kept researching, beyond the *Merck* and into the relevant case studies, which gave me some hope, and so I tried to give Catrine some hope, too, even though she didn't ask for any, didn't seem to need any, either. I told her about the woman in Wichita who'd had a hole in her heart, too, a big hole, and she lived until she was ninety-two. I told her about the man in Marblehead who'd done a triathlon a year, for twenty years, after he'd learned about the hole in his heart, and died only because one day he was biking too early in the morning in too-dark clothing and was hit by a car. "If you don't bike too early in the morning, or if you wear light-colored clothes if you do," I told her, "you could live forever."

"Could, could, could," Catrine said, then put her inhaler to her mouth, aimed it at me like a weapon, and sucked.

I knew where this was headed, or should have. Because this is what I did and do, at Kodak and elsewhere: I researched. For instance, Catrine is from Montreal, and when I met her ten years ago and fell in love, I did heavy research on the city: its history, its customs, its civic institutions and festivals, its restaurants, its average high temperature and snowfall, its biggest employers, and its general feeling about the Quebec question and whether or not to separate from the rest of Canada. I walked around, citing obscure facts about Catrine's hometown, facts she didn't care about and was unimpressed by, and one day, when I was telling her about the origin of Montreal bagels and how they're different from what we, as Americans, know bagels to be, she said, "Eric, why are you doing this?"

"Because I love you. Because I want to know everything about you."

"That's sweet," she said. "But cut it out."

And this is what she told me, more or less, two weeks before we ended up going to the Lizzie Borden Bed and Breakfast, too. It was a Saturday, in the afternoon, and Catrine was taking a nap, was sleeping soundly, too soundly as far as I was concerned, and I thought, *Oh Jesus, has it happened? Has it happened already?* Because I knew from my research that people with this hole in their heart often died in their sleep, and I leaned over Catrine's body, desperate to hear her heart beating, desperate to hear and feel the flutter of her breath, and I must have gotten too close, because Catrine said, without opening her eyes, "I'm still alive."

"Of course you are," I said.

"Leave me alone," she said. "If you love me, you'll leave me alone."

"I can do that," I said.

Except I couldn't. Because at night, when I was trying to sleep next to her—and when I was at work, trying to test the prototype developing solution I was supposed to be testing— all I could think of was this big hole in Catrine's heart; all I could hear was the big hole talking to me, saying, "She will die, and you will never forget about her. You will never love anyone as much as you love her. You will never stop missing her." And the big hole in Catrine's heart also told me, "Do not leave her alone. Bad things will happen if you leave her alone." Soon, I was following her everywhere—around the house, in the yard; I even took a sick day or two so that I could follow her in my car when she ran errands and such. And on the Friday Catrine kicked me out, I'd followed her to the grocery store, I was tailing her down the frozen foodstuffs aisle, and she wheeled her and her half-full cart around and said, "Get out."

"Of the grocery store?" I asked.

"Of the house," she said. "Do it. Now."

Which was how and why I ended up staying at the Budget Inn on Alexander for six days. The Budget Inn was a mile or so from my house, but even there, I could hear the big hole in Catrine's heart talking to me, and it wouldn't shut up, and I called Catrine every night, begging her to let me come home, and each night she said, "Not yet, not yet," until finally she called and asked me to come with her to the Lizzie Borden Bed and Breakfast, and I agreed.

AFTER AN HOUR, we have gone through the parlor, the sitting room, the dining room, the kitchen, and Mr. and Mrs. Borden's downstairs bedroom. I have an idea why the chainsmoker is here: because she knows everything possible about the case and wants confirmation of what she already knows. I know why Mr. and Mrs. Ohio are here: because they visit every historical home that they can, because historical homes are more boring then they are, and this makes them feel better and interesting in comparison. I know why the fraternity boys are here: they've been duped. I know why the tour guide is here: it's her job. But I still have no idea why Catrine and I are here; she's by my side now again, with her hand in my back pocket, the way they do in jeans commercials, the way she hasn't done ever, and I have no idea why she's doing that, either.

"Concerning Mr. Borden," the tour guide tells us, "he was notoriously stingy with his considerable fortune. He gave Lizzie—*his grown daughter*—a small allowance. A *very* small allowance." Here she looks at us meaningfully, over her bi-focals, as if the cheapskates among us should adopt more high-rolling ways before, we, too, get our whacks with the axe. The Ohio woman glances knowingly at her husband, who looks away sheepishly. I think I know why: we've paid two hundred and fifty dollars for one night in the Andrew and Abby Suite, which is basically two small rooms—one room with a double bed and a musty comforter, and one with a rickety antique desk and a mannequin dressed like Lizzie in period dress and a fragile-looking fainting couch, which, if someone were to faint on it, might itself suffer a serious collapse—and no private bathroom, and if my wife had wanted me to go to this place and I weren't trying to get into her good graces and she weren't dying, I might have complained about how expensive it was, too.

"Tell us about the number of whacks with an axe Lizzie actually gave her father," the lesbian chain-smoker says. She's calmed down considerably, and her hatred for the fraternity boys has become noticeably low-grade, like a cold you get used to. As for the boys themselves, they know now that they are not in the childhood home of their favorite lesbian porn star, but they also know that they are in the home of a possible lesbian axe murder, and this has taken some of the sting out of their disappointment.

"Concerning the famous forty whacks with an axe," the tour guide says, "this, of course, is what the famous rhyme tells us." And here she recites the famous rhyme, which says, basically, that Mr. Borden was killed by forty whacks with an axe, and then adds: "Mr. Borden, in reality, only received twenty-eight whacks . . ."

"Still," the fat fraternity boy says. "Ouch."

". . . but for the sake of the rhyme, twenty-eight became forty."

"But hey," the thin fraternity boy says, "it's 'whacks' that rhymes with 'axe.' The number of whacks doesn't matter." Everyone looks at him in huge surprise, even his buddy, which makes me realize I wasn't the only one thinking ungenerous thoughts about him paying attention in his English class. "What?" he says. "They *don't*."

The tour guide stares at him down her beakish nose for an extra beat and then returns to the automatic pilot of her tour guiding. "Concerning the famous picture of Lizzie at the trial," she says, and then moves to the next room, the living room, where, on the wall, next to the pictures of the half dozen not-exactly-famous actresses who have portrayed Lizzie in the movies, on TV, and in the theater, is the artistic rendering of Lizzie at her trial—grim-faced, defiant, strong. She looks strong; that's the thing I really notice, and maybe this is why we're here: because Catrine wants to be inspired by the example of a strong woman who faced adversity and survived, even if the woman is an axe murderer and the adversity is her axe-murdering. Even if this is the case, I am all for it, and we can spend the rest of our lives going to the historical homes of other famously strong women who faced adversity and survived—Susan B. Anthony, Rosa Parks, Annie Oakley. If strong women are what Catrine wants, then strong women are what she'll get.

Except she doesn't. Catrine looks at the picture for a second and says, "Huh," then lets go of my hand and walks out of the living room and back to the parlor, where we've already spent a long half hour, and where there is only the couch where they found Mr. Borden's bloody and perforated body. This is what Catrine has been doing throughout the entire tour: she keeps floating in and out of the rooms, the way the tour guide said the ghost of Lizzie did during the filming of an upcoming episode of *Unsolved Mysteries*. Catrine seems to be everywhere the rest of the tour is not, and now I can hear her in the parlor, sucking on her inhaler, sucking on it hard, maybe too hard, and maybe something is wrong. I take a step to follow her, but then I hear her voice saying, "Leave me alone," and "Get out," and that voice is as scary as the voice of her heart's hole, saying, "She will die, she will die."

So I leave her alone, in the parlor, and stay where I am, in the living room. The tour guide and the chain-smoker are still talking about the famous trial—the tour guide has told us nothing about the trial except that it was famous, and thus far the tour has been composed of random conjectures beginning with the word "concerning"—but the fraternity boys, they've disengaged themselves from the subject of Lizzie *and* Lezzie Borden, and have engaged the Ohioans in a conversation about weight loss and gain, and in specifically, Mrs. Ohio's long history of failed diets.

"I've tried everything," she said. "All meat, no meat. Full fructose saturation. You name it."

"Everything except exercise," Mr. Ohio mutters. He must realize what he's said and how awful it sounds, because immediately his albino-blue eyes get watery and he bites his lip ruefully and adds, "Because of her hip."

"What about your hip?" the fat fraternity boy says.

"It's bad," she says. "Arthritic. I'll have to replace it. But first, the doctor says I have to lose some weight, which is difficult to do because I can't exercise, because of my hip."

"Now that," the thin fraternity boy says, "is a *quandary*."

"It makes you think," the husband says, and shakes his head wisely, and you know he's the sort of man who gets philosophical after visiting aged relatives in nursing homes and makes big statements about how some things are worse than death and how, if he ever gets like Great-Aunt So-and-So, to just kill him. "I mean it," I can hear him saying. Earlier I saw his wife eyeing Lizzie's famous axe head in its glass case, and so maybe she was anticipating his request and the way she might honor it.

"I'm on this diet that you should try," the fat boy says to Mrs. Ohio, and suddenly he becomes the very sincere, caring boy his mother probably raised him to be and loved. "I don't eat anything that begins with the letter *C*."

"Dude," his buddy says. "That diet is bullshit."

The tour guide hears this, interrupts the chain-smoker's theory about Lizzie Borden's guilt in the court of popular opinion, and says, "Concerning Mr. Borden and obscenity, he had quite a . . ." And here she pauses, as if searching for the right word, although you have the sense this pause, too, is a rehearsed part of her tour-guiding, to make it seem less rehearsed. "Mouth," she finally says. "But he would not tolerate cursing on the part of his daughters. Simply would not tolerate it."

"Simply would not tolerate it," the chain-smoker repeats.

"Concerning Lizzie and cursing," the tour guide says, "once, when she was twenty-three, she used a curse word—no one knows which one—and Mr. Borden paddled her."

"With a paddle?" the thin boy asks.

"Bad move, Dad," the fat one says.

"Concerning the paddle," the tour guide says, "rumor has it, Lizzie took the paddle afterward and threw it into the central fireplace, which, as we know, was used to heat the entire house and so was very hot. She did this right in front of Mr. Borden."

"Threw it in the central fireplace," the chain-smoker says.

"That should have been a red signal to old Dad," the fat frat boy says.

"Red light," the thin one says.

"Dad should have done his *research*," I say, surprising myself and everyone else, too. They all look at me in complete confusion, and so I add, "He should have done his research on *daughters*." At this, Catrine pops her head into the living room. She has a funny, satisfied-but-tired look on her face—somewhere between fatigue and love—but before I can tell what she's learned in the parlor and what she hasn't, what sort of *research* she's done in there and whether it has made her happy or unhappy, before I can yell, "Come back, come back. I miss you," she disappears from the doorway again, and the tour guide takes us upstairs, to where Lizzie's stepmother slept those many years ago and where we're sleeping tonight.

CONCERNING RESEARCH, WHEN Catrine told me that she wanted to go the Lizzie Borden Bed and Breakfast in Fall River, Massachusetts, I didn't ask her why, per her request. Instead, I went to work, got on the computer, and researched Fall River itself, its main immigrant groups (Portuguese) and industry (shipping), and of course I also researched Lizzie Borden, her birth mother (who died when she was a girl), who she was accused of murdering (her father and stepmother), whether the axe used to murder them was ever found (the handle was not, but the axe head was), whether she was found guilty or innocent (the latter), and why the case continues to attract the attracted (because no one knows whether she really did do it or not, because there was never any other suspect, because the case is as mysterious now as it was then).

Why did I do this? Because at Kodak, at our new employee training seminar, they taught us that if you look hard enough, you will find something you are looking for, some-times without even knowing you're looking for it. If you look hard enough, you will find something that is useful, something that will help you, and thus something that will help Kodak.

But what if it doesn't? What if this is true only of film and film-related products? Because I have done my research, have paid close attention as we strolled from bedroom to bedroom; I have felt Lizzie's bedspread ("Concerning the bedspread," the tour guide tells us, "it's not the actual bedspread but a close reproduction; feel it"), looked through her now-empty closet, flushed the toilet in the hallway bathroom, and then flushed it again; I've watched Catrine flit in and out of my line of vi-sion, from room to room, have tried to discern some meaning behind her flitting, some message or signal. And what have I found? What has my research and my looking earned me? Nothing. And now we're in our room, the last room of the tour, the room where the stepmother was killed. Our bag is on the fainting couch, our clothes draped over the chair and desk and bed, and it looks much like our bedroom at home, where I have also looked and researched and found nothing useful, nothing that will help us.

"Concerning the stepmother," the tour guide says, "she was sleeping at the time of her demise. And since this was in the summer, and it was hot, and it was a time before window screens . . ."

"Back in the day," the thin fraternity boy says.

". . . people slept in tents of netting. To escape the mosquitoes."

"To escape the mosquitoes," the chain-smoker repeats.

"Concerning the netting," the tour guide says, "whoever killed the second Mrs. Borden chopped right through the netting on the way to the second Mrs. Borden."

"Swiss cheese," the fat fraternity boy says, and then, anticipating our bewildered looks, says, "Holes in the netting *and* the second Mrs. Borden. Swiss cheese."

"Concerning Swiss cheese," the tour guide says, "there are snacks in the kitchen downstairs." Everyone except me applauds, as if they've gotten exactly what they came for, and the tour guide takes a little bow, her arms flat against the top of her high-waisted skirt, before walking down the stairs. We all follow her, even Catrine, who appears suddenly from another room and silently takes my hand as we descend the stairs. Since the staircase is narrow, she is close, so close her arm and hip are rubbing against me. She smiles, looks like she's happy to be rubbing up against me, although I don't know why and I don't ask. I don't ask where she's been or why she's been floating from one room to the other instead of sticking with the rest of the tour. I don't ask any of the questions I want to ask, such as: Why are we here? What am I supposed to have learned, and how can it save us? I don't ask anything, don't know anything, either, except what I knew before tonight, which is this: Catrine will die, and I will be alone and I will never love anyone as much as I love her and I will never stop missing her. That is all I know—that and how the rest of the night will unfold. We will eat a cracker or two in the kitchen to be polite, and because I know I won't sleep, I will drink one cup of coffee, then another, and I'll feel my heart racing and I will want it to get louder and stronger and bigger until it cannot be contained by its cavity, until it gets so big that it will leave my body and surround us, protect us, the way the mosquito netting was supposed to protect the second Mrs. Borden but didn't. Then Catrine and I will go to our room, the room where the second Mrs. Borden was killed, where Catrine will sleep and I will watch her. After a half hour, I will want to wake her, to make sure she's alive, to make sure she hasn't left me yet. But I won't wake her; I won't. I will stay on my side of the bed, and from there I will try to listen to her heart and I will let her sleep.

# Good Night

............................................................

**A**nd even after all that, even after everything I'd said to him earlier, he still came to say good night before he went to bed, the way he had every night, pretty much, since he was a little boy. He wasn't a little boy anymore, fourteen years old and taller than I am, and I say this not by way of bragging, because I'm not that tall. Anyway, he knocked on the bathroom door. I was brushing my teeth, and said through my mouthful of paste, "Yeah?" I spat into the sink, and when I turned around he was standing there in the doorway. He was bare-chested, wearing the sweatpants he wore to bed every night, which were not much distinguishable from the sweatpants he wore to school every day. This was one of the things we tended to argue about, although I can't remember if that was one of the things we had just argued about or not. We might have argued about the way his armpits or breath stunk, or why he chewed his fingernails so incessantly, or why he then put those chewed-off fingernails in his shirt and pants and coat pockets, or whether he was planning on *saving* his chewed-off fingernails for some special occasion, or whether he was capable of telling me the date and time of that special occasion, or whether he was capable of communicating in something other than one-word sentences, or why he didn't look me in the eye, or why he was so weird sometimes, or whether he was not actually weird but rather living in another universe, not a distant universe, just a universe, say, five seconds behind our own, because why else did it take such an odd amount of time for him to respond to the questions I asked him, any question, like "Do you have any homework?" questions that weren't tough, not even if you were a moron, which was another thing we sometimes argued about, whether he was a moron or not. "I just wanted to say good night," he said, looking from the floor, his sky-blue eyes trying to meet mine, and I thought, not for the first time, not even for the first time that day, or hour, *Oh God, what is wrong with me? You're such a sweet kid. I love you so much,* and I took two quick steps forward and hugged him, and he hugged me back, sort of. I mean he put his left arm around me, but he kept his right hand up, sort of pushing at my chest with it, making it hard for me to hug him back, even with both arms, which was what I was trying to do. Had he always hugged like that? Would he always hug like that? What kind of person hugs like that? These, I knew, were exactly the things I *shouldn't* say, and I almost didn't.

# Our Pointy Boots

The reporters stand between us and our transport; they put their microphones and cameras in our faces and say, "You're going home for Christmas. What's the first thing you're going to do when you get home?"

We ask, "What are our choices?"

"The usual two," the reporters say. "Are you going to hold your sweet babies real tight? Or are you going to lay your fallen comrade to rest while the chaplain conveys the gratitude of the president and the entire nation and then prays to God for the state of your comrade's immortal soul?" Then they consult their notes and ask, "You do have a fallen comrade, don't you?"

"Yes," we say. "Sanders."

"Well," they say. "What's the first thing you're going to do when you get home? Are you going to bury him? Or are your going to hold your sweet babies real tight?"

"Neither," we tell them. "The first thing we're going to do

when we get home is put on our pointy boots and parade around the Public Square."

BEFORE WE GRADUATED from high school, before we met and married our sweet babies, before we had babies with our sweet babies, before we got the jobs that we didn't want to work at for the rest of our lives, before we realized that we probably *would* work at them for the rest of our lives if we didn't do something about it, before we did something about it and joined up, before we went to Iraq, before what happened to Sanders, before any of this happened, we were sitting around on a Friday just before graduation, skipping school which, as graduating seniors, we were of course expected to do, feeling bored, feeling like we were missing something in our lives. And so we decided to go to the Public Square, to the Bon-Ton, which had a little of everything, to see if they had what we were missing.

They were terrified of us at the Bon-Ton. Because we were young and noisy, and we seemed even noisier than we were because we were the only customers in the store, because the store was the only store left on the Public Square that hadn't pulled out and moved to the mall, and because we couldn't, at first, find what we were missing, and this disappointed us and so we let them know about it. They tried to sell us fedoras in the Men's Department, and we put our fists through their tops and then wore them around our wrists like bracelets. They tried to sell us stirrup pants in the Ladies' Department, and we said stirrup pants were an abomination and so we liberated the stirrups with our hands and feet and teeth, and then reshelved what remained with the other, normal pants, thus diminishing all of their retail value. They tried to sell us nonstick pans in Housewares, and we took the pans in one hand and took the gum out of our mouths with the other and stuck the gum to the nonstick pans and then wondered what the people at the Bon-Ton would have to say about *that*. The people at the Bon-Ton didn't have anything to say; they scattered, hiding in dressing rooms and locking the slatted doors behind them; or crouching behind checkout counters, armed only with their bar code guns. And so there was no one to help us when we entered Footwear and saw the rows and rows of boots, their pointy toes pointing at us, as if to say they wanted us as much as we, we realized, wanted them.

ONCE WE'VE FINISHED talking to the reporters, we get on the transport that takes us to Germany and then another one that takes home. We get off the transport, and there, standing on the base's tarmac, are our sweet babies, waving at us. We can see that our sweet babies don't have our babies with them, for which we are grateful. The tarmac has been cleared, but the snowbanks surrounding it are ten, fifteen feet high, high enough so that you can't see the electric fences somewhere on the other side of them. It's sunny out, the sky is crystal blue, but it's so, so cold that our eyes start to water immediately, the way they did when we first got to the desert and sand got into our eyes and they started to water immediately. This is one of the things we've learned: not that people are the same wherever you go, but that we don't change, no matter where we are. We shoulder our duffel bags and walk toward our sweet babies. As we get closer, our sweet babies stop waving, run toward us, arms out in front of them, preparing to hold us. Their faces look hopeful but nervous. Because they know that Sanders is dead, and they also know about the usual choices, know that we could choose him instead of them. When they get close enough, they put their arms around us and hold us real tight. But we don't hold them back. We keep one arm to our side; the other holds on to our duffels. When our sweet babies realize this, they push themselves away, like they're the ship and we're the shore.

"You bastard," our sweet babies say to those of us who are men. "You bitch," our sweet babies say to those of us who are women. "You chose Sanders, didn't you? You chose burying Sanders over holding us real tight."

"We didn't choose Sanders," we say.

"Well, you obviously didn't choose us," they say.

"That's true," we say.

They look at us, confusion displacing anger on their faces for a second before they figure out what's going on, before they figure out what we've chosen. "Oh no," they say.

"Oh yes," we say. And then we ask them to please take us home, where our pointy boots are in our closets, waiting for us to put them on and parade around the Public Square.

WE HAVE SEEN and done some things: when we first killed an enemy, we were glad, because for the first time ever we found that we could actually do what we were trained to do; when we first killed someone who we weren't sure was an enemy, we were happy that the word "enemy" existed so that we could call him one anyway; when we first saw one of our own comrades killed, we were ecstatic that it wasn't us; when we first saw one of our own comrades killed by a bullet that might have been fired by one of us, we were angry he was dead so he couldn't exonerate us, unless one of us had actually killed him, and then we were grateful he wasn't alive to say so. We've seen and done all of that. Plus, there's Sanders. But we're truly ashamed of only one thing: that when we first saw the pointy boots in the Bon-Ton, we had a fight over what kind we should get.

Those of us who grew up on a farm refused to buy Luccheses, for fearing of being mistaken for wops. Those of us who were Italians refused to buy Fryes, for fear of being mistaken for rednecks. Some of us didn't want to get Acmes, because they sounded like joke boots. Some of us didn't want to get Bear-paws, because the name was too close to that of the pastry. Some of us had no trouble getting Durangos, except for those of us who had trucks that went by the same name. We all, finally, agreed on Sanders, except for Sanders, who said it was a stupid name for a boot. It was like giving a dog a human name, he said. "I would never name *my* dog Sanders," one of us said, and then Sanders wanted to know what the hell *that* was supposed to mean. And how does life turn out this way? How does the thing that promises to be different, the thing that promises to make you feel good, end up making you feel as bad as everything else? And when that happens, do you take it out on the thing that has promised so much, or do you take it out on yourself for believing the promise?

We did both: we took it out on ourselves, and the boots. We hurled them at each other, at close range; we gouged each others' eyes with the pointy toes; we clubbed each other with the hard heels; we put the boots over our hands, like gloves, and then boxed each other with them; we fell on the floor and wept at how pathetic and ridiculous we had become, how pathetic and ridiculous we always had been and always would be. And then, after we wept but before we could figure out what else to do that we might later weep over, we were quiet, just for a moment, just long enough to hear one of the salesladies say meekly from inside her locked, slatted dressing room door: "What I'm hearing is that it doesn't really matter what *kind* of boots you're wearing, just as long as they're pointy."

It was like hearing the voice of God: not a vengeful God, but a practical, reasonable God, a God who didn't keep tabs on all the bad things you did, but who listened, really listened to you while you did those bad things, so as to help you get what you wanted so you'd stop doing them. When you hear that voice, you don't stop and ask how it got so wise, or question its wisdom. You just do what it tells you to do. We did what the saleslady told us to do. We gathered up the boots, found their partners. We located our size and our preferred brand and put them on, no matter how damaged they were, how damaged we had made them. We returned the boots we didn't want to their boxes and put the boxes back on the shelves. Then we lined up and proceeded past the locked dressing room doors; as we went past the saleslady's door, we put our mouths to the slats and thanked her for her help. "I guess you're welcome," was her blessing. And then we left the Bon-Ton and went out onto the Public Square.

ONCE OUR SWEET babies figure out what we've chosen, they say, to themselves, "Poor Sanders. Poor us." And then to us: "You fuckers can just go ahead and walk home," and then they run to their cars and lay rubber out of the parking lot before we can force our way into the cars. So, we reshoulder our duffel bags and start walking.

Just outside the base, on the other side of the street from the entrance gate, are two protestors. They are both dressed head to toe in insulated camo, layers and layers of it, with only their faces uncovered. One, a woman, her cheeks round and fiery red, her gray hair peeking out from under her camo ski hat, is holding a cardboard sign with the words NO MORE WAR written on it in red marker, with a green peace symbol drawn underneath. The other protestor is a man. Ice hangs from his gray beard, and snot from his red nose, like Christmas tree ornaments. He chants, *"No more war!"* into a bullhorn, drowning out whatever it is the woman is chanting, which is also probably *"No more war!"* They are exactly like us: there should be more of them, and they should have better ideas, and they should have better ways to tell people about their ideas. When they see us walk out of the gate, they stop chanting and come over to talk with us.

"Welcome home," the guy with the bullhorn says, although not through the bullhorn, which he's holstered. The holster looks to be made out of an enormous widemouthed wine sack, held in place by an orange power cord around the guy's waist. Instead of a normal belt buckle, this is held in place by the cord's prongs and holes. There are other wine-sack-looking vessels of various sizes attached to the cord, spaced a few inches apart. One is holding a thermos. One is holding a cell phone. One is holding something that actually does look like it might contain wine but is probably only a hot water bottle. One is holding something in tinfoil, probably lunch. We've never seen anything like it.

"Would you look at those holsters," we say.

"Well, I made them myself," the guy says, obviously so proud. He seems like he's on the verge of telling us all about how he made them and why when the woman, who is probably his wife, who has probably heard about this guy's home-made holsters a thousand times, interrupts and says, "We're proud of you. We feel it's important you know that."

"OK," we say.

"This"—and here she taps her sign with the hand that's not holding it—"this doesn't mean we're not proud of you."

"Thank you," we say.

"We know *you* don't want to be there any more than *we* want you to," she says.

"But we volunteered," we say.

"You didn't think you were volunteering for this," she says. She looks at her sign and points to the word WAR, so we know exactly what's she's talking about.

"What *did* we think we were volunteering for, then?" we ask. We know the answer, and she doesn't, but even if she did, she'd look at us the way she looks at us now—in huge disappointment, as though we're not the people she thought we were, not the people she needs us to be. Still, she's not quite ready to give up on us. We know this, because we know her. She really is the kind of person who wants to give peace a chance, and since she's giving peace a chance, she figures she might as well give us one, too. *"We,"* she says. "You keep talking about yourselves as 'We,' and not 'I.' You poor people. I bet the Army taught you to talk like that, to think like that."

"Actually," we tell her, "we've talked and thought this way ever since the day we first put on our pointy boots and paraded around the Public Square."

"What?" she says, but she doesn't wait for any answer. She slowly backs away from us, to across the street, where she stands holding her sign over her chest with both hands, as though out of modesty. "Are you coming, Harold?" she shouts. But Harold is not coming, not quite yet.

"Tell us something about what it's like over there," he says eagerly. We know him, too. He's the kind of guy—with his camo, his questions, his bullhorn, his homemade holsters, his gear—who spends every minute he's not protesting the war fantasizing about what it's like to be in one. "Tell us something we might not have heard from someone else."

"Well," we say, "one of the things you might not have heard is that when we're interrogating someone we say that if they don't tell us what we want to know, we'll cut off their heads and then fuck their skulls."

"Always?" Harold asks.

"Every time," we say.

"Has anyone ever told you what you wanted to know?"

"No," we say.

"I wouldn't think so," he says, then glances at those of us who are women, then looks away from them before they see him looking. It's too late; they see.

"What?" those of us who are women say. "You got some kind of problem?"

"No, no problem," the guy says, his hand moving instinctively to the bullhorn in his holster. "I just have a hard time imagining it, that's all."

"You have a hard time imagining us saying that we'd cut off someone's head and fuck their skull?"

"No, I can imagine you *saying* it. But can, you know, a gal actually do that? I mean, physically?"

"Harold, put a sock in it," his wife says from across the street.

"You should listen to your wife, Harold," those of us who are women say.

"You should listen to those of us who are women, Harold," those of us who are men say. But he doesn't listen to any of us.

"I mean, it's not much of a threat, is it?"

"*That's* it," those of us who are women say. They drop their duffel bags and charge Harold. Those of us who are men have to restrain them while he retreats across the street. He stands next to his wife and shouts through his bullhorn, "It's kind of funny, if you think about it," and then his wife snatches the bullhorn out of his hands and tucks it into her parka.

"Sanders wouldn't have thought it was funny," we say.

"Who is Sanders?" Harold's wife wants to know.

"Sanders is dead," we say. "We're going to lay him to rest tomorrow."

"I bet Sanders didn't think he was volunteering for *that*," the woman says.

"No, he didn't," we say as we start walking home. Because we know what Sanders thought he was volunteering for. He thought he was volunteering for the same thing we did: for the chance to feel the way we felt when we first put on our pointy boots and paraded around the Public Square.

IT WAS LUNCHTIME when we got out of the Bon-Ton and onto the Public Square. It was sunny, hot, almost summer. The county courthouse workers were sitting in the shadow of the statue of our locally significant Revolutionary

War general with their bagged lunches, struggling to unwrap their cellophane-wrapped meat-and-cheese sandwiches. The guys from the halfway house were lying back-down and shirtless on the grass, wolfing down their cigarettes and then lighting their new butts with the remainder of the old without once opening their eyes. The bail bondsmen stood near their storefronts, sipping burnt coffee out of their Styrofoam cups, eyeing the cuffed as they were led into the courthouse, making bets on how much their bail would be, on who would end up jumping and who would not.

And then there was us, fifteen teenagers, boys and girls, standing in front of the Bon-Ton. For a while, we did nothing but look down and admire our new pointy boots. There is no love so true as one's love for one's new pair of shoes, and we loved our pointy boots even more truly than that. We turned our feet this way and that, watched as the boots glinted in the sun; we squatted down and traced our fingers over the stitched patterns, or, if we'd chosen boots with no patterns, we ran our fingers over the smooth, stitchless surfaces; we stuck our toes into the smallest sidewalk cracks and marveled at how pointy the toes really were. We looked around the Square, and saw that no one else was wearing anything remotely like them. We pitied these people. Because this is what it means to be in love: you feel sorry for people who aren't. And then you feel happy that no one feels sorry for you. You feel so happy that it's not enough to just sit there and admire the beloved. You have to do something that shows the beloved how much you love it.

And if you love your pointy boots the way we loved ours, you show them so by parading in them around the Public Square.

We did that. We proceeded loosely, not in formation as we learned to do later at the base; not single file, or on our hands and knees, as we learned to do in the desert; but some of us in twos and threes, some of us by ourselves, some of us stopping, momentarily, to admire our boots in the windows of the empty storefronts, or to wipe some dust or dirt off of our pointy boots, and then moving on again. Around and around we went. We did it for the joy of the thing, and not necessarily to be noticed by the poor people who were not us. But they noticed us anyway. The county courthouse workers looked away from their sandwiches; the bail bondsman, from those who might soon be bail bonded. The guys from the halfway house actually sat up and opened their eyes and let their butts die out without lighting another one. One of the most fully gone of the halfway house guys even got up and started parading with us. He wore sweatpants, with one sweatpant leg down to the ankle, the other pushed up to the knee, and beat-up white leather high-top basketball sneakers with no socks. He brought his knees up high as he marched, and waved his unlit cigarette like a baton. He was mocking us, probably, and we let him, rather than kicking his ass, which we could have done, easily. We could have kicked his ass, no problem. But instead, we practiced restraint. We figured ass-kicking was unnecessary, figured he'd get tired and sooner or later return to the grass with his halfway house brothers. Which is exactly what happened. After a lap or two around the Square, he went back to the grass and sat down and watched us. Everyone did. We knew what they were seeing: they were seeing fifteen teenagers, some boys, some girls, parading together but not together, all wearing pointy boots but not the same pointy boots. Fifteen individuals but also a group, a group people could identify and admire: those kids who paraded around the Public Square in their pointy boots. They could see what we—and they, and everyone—were told in school was all around us: a nation of individuals, united. They could see the promise of America, in other words, made flesh by us and our pointy boots.

IT'S DARK BY the time we get home. We knock on our front doors, and our sweet babies unlock them and let us in. But before we're able to get our boots out of our closets and on our feet and start parading around the Public Square, our sweet babies try to stop us. We keep trying to go to the bedroom, to the closet where our pointy boots are waiting for us, and our sweet babies keep edging in front of us, keeping between us and the room, asking us questions. They ask us if we want something to eat. They ask if we want to take a rest, or watch some TV, or maybe play a board game. They ask us to admire the Christmas tree (there is a Christmas tree, in the corner, next to the TV, a pretty, droopy Scotch pine with colored lights and presents piled underneath it and a wooden Nativity scene with baby Jesus and his mom and dad facing outward and the donkeys and wise men facing the presents).

They tell us that they were waiting for us to get home to put the star on the top of the tree. They produce the star, which is silver and which they've been hiding behind their backs. They ask us if we'd like to put the star on the top of the tree now or a little bit later. Because a little bit later would be fine, they tell us. "Why don't we do it a little bit later?" our sweet babies say. But for right now, would we like some hot chocolate? We know what they're doing. We know they've taken a seminar, at the base, about what to do when your soldier comes home. We know they've been warned to expect us to be a little different. To be a little *off.* We know they've been told to be patient with us, to not force us to talk about things we might not want to talk about. We know they've been told to be solicitous, to *ask* us what we'd like to do and not *tell* us. We know they've been reminded they have only two weeks with us before we're shipped back, and not to ruin our little time together by trying to rush things. We know this because we were made to take a seminar at the base in Iraq, telling us to expect the same thing about ourselves, to treat ourselves with the same caution, the same care.

When we don't answer any of their questions, our sweet babies put their hands on our shoulders and look into our eyes and say, "We missed you."

"Yes," we say.

"I bet you miss Sanders," they say.

"Yes," we say.

"Poor Sanders," they say.

"Yes," we say. And then: "About those pointy boots . . ."

*"Fine,"* they say. They take their hands off our shoulders, step to the side, and make a sweeping motion with their arms in the direction of the bedroom, the closet, the boots, as if to say, *It's all yours.* We can see the hurt on their faces. We can see what we've done to them, what we've always done to them. We are not heartless, and to show we're not heartless, we say, "Sorry."

"You've always cared more about your pointy boots than you've cared about us, haven't you?" they ask.

"Yes," we say, and run past them into the bedroom.


AT THE END of lunch hour, the county workers finished their sandwiches and went back into the courthouse. The bail bondsmen finished their coffee and went back into their storefronts. The halfway house guys finished their cigarettes and went back into their halfway houses. And we finished our parading and sat down at the foot of the statue of our local Revolutionary War general. We'd paraded for almost an hour, but we didn't feel at all tired, not even our feet, which would have been expected, considering we'd been parading in brand-new pointy boots. But we didn't have one blister, one strained arch, one bruised heel, one rubbed-raw toe. We felt *good.* And if we felt so good, some of us wondered, if we weren't tired, if we weren't footsore, then what did we think we were doing, sitting down? "Let's get up and *parade*, for crying out loud," some of us said. But others of us said no. Because hadn't we felt good before? Hadn't we felt good on the basketball court, or smoking cigarettes behind the art room, or drinking beer on the dirt roads outside town while sitting on the hoods of our parents' second cars, or doing things to each other in the cornfields next to the dirt roads that we'd always wanted to do but couldn't get up the nerve to without the help of the beer? And hadn't we then ruined those good things? Hadn't we then taken and missed a terrible shot we had no business taking at exactly the worst possible moment and lost the game, or smoked an extra cigarette and got caught doing it by the art teacher, or drank ten beers too many and then later wrecked our parents' cars, or, before we wrecked those cars, done things we shouldn't have with each other in the cornfields and then regretted it afterward? Hadn't we ruined good things before? some of us asked. And it should be said that Sanders was one of us who asked it. You would think, after everything that had happened, that Sanders would have been one of us who wanted to get up and parade and ruin our good feeling, but no: he was one of us who spoke eloquently about not ruining it. He was one of us who said that we should always keep the memory, the vision, of our parading around the Square in our pointy boots, but we shouldn't ruin it by going out and parading in our pointy boots around the Public Square whenever we felt a little sad, a little lonely, a little useless. He said that we should try to find that feeling somewhere else—through our work, through our marriages, through *whatever*—that we should go looking for that feeling everywhere. And even if we never found it, even if our lives ended up as lousy as they had been before we put on our pointy boots, then at least we'd have the memory of that time when it wasn't lousy, when we felt *good*; at least we'd have the memory of the one good thing we *didn't* ruin. And no matter what, we should agree to do this together, to do everything together, as one: we should marry our sweet babies as one, join up as one, speak as one, remember our parading and our pointy boots as one. Then those of us who hadn't wanted to parade again asked, "Agreed?" And those of us who had wanted to parade again said, "Agreed." Then we went home and took off our pointy boots and put them in our closets. We polished them regularly, religiously, treated them more tenderly, more lovingly, than we ever did our sweet babies, which our sweet babies never failed to notice and comment upon. Whenever we moved, we took the boots with us, moved them from bedroom closet to bedroom closet, but we never put them on again, not once, until now.

WE'RE SITTING ON our beds, trying to put on our pointy boots, when our sweet babies peek their heads into our bedrooms. They have crazed, determined I'm-going-to-try-one-more-time smiles on their faces. "I have a surprise for you," each of them says, then their faces disappear again. We don't respond. We just sit there, on our beds, trying to put on our pointy boots. This is difficult, more difficult than we remember, more difficult than it used to be, because our feet have been in round-toed boots for so long they've stopped being the kind of feet that will slip easily into pointy boots. A few seconds later, we hear soft, muffled, thumping coming toward us. Then the sounds stop. We look up and see our sweet babies standing in the doorway, and in front of them, in front of us, our babies. They're wearing overlarge T-shirts that read DADDY'S LITTLE GIRL, or MOMMY'S LITTLE BOY, or DADDY'S LITTLE BOY, or MOMMY'S LITTLE GIRL, depending. The lettering on the shirt is brightly colored and badly written, as though actually written by children who are only eighteen months old, which is how old our babies are. They're so much bigger than the last time we saw them; they hardly even look like our babies anymore. Our babies turn to look at our sweet babies, who nod; our babies turn back to us and wave with their white, sticky, pudgy fingers. They smile at us in their shy, distracted, happy way. We knew this was going to happen. On the transport, we warned each other about this moment, the moment when our babies would be produced, when our babies and sweet babies would conspire to melt our hearts. "Be strong," we told each other on the transport. We reminded each other that our hearts had melted when our babies had first been born, too. We reminded each other of how we had each said to our newborn babies, "You are mine. You are mine and you melted my heart, and I will never let you down." And then, of course, we did let them down, in thousands of small and large ways, every day of their lives, including by leaving them to go to Iraq. We resented them because of it—there is no resentment so pure as that for the people who you love and who you have let down, and our resentment was even purer than that, because we were comparing our babies to our pointy boots, who we had never let down after we'd first put them on and who we had never resented—and our hearts hardened; they became even harder than before, to compensate for melting in the first place, for believing that our babies could make us feel as purely good as our pointy boots had. "There is no sense going through all that again," we told each other on the transport. We look away from our babies and pull even harder on our boots, trying to jam our feet into them.

"Don't you want to hold your baby?" our sweet babies ask as we pull and grunt, pull and grunt. We look at our babies again, almost involuntarily. They're closer now. They are on the verge of calling to us by name, or at least by title. Their lips open and close, open and close, as though practicing to say the word. It is almost impossible to resist a baby who is on the verge of saying your name for the first time. Still, we resist. Still, we struggle with the boots. Still, we don't talk to our babies. Still, we do not move to hold our babies. This infuriates our sweet babies; this *pisses them off.* They pick up our babies and pull them away from us, to their chests, as though we're not worthy of them. This is another thing the seminars have taught them: that they will become infuriated by us; it's inevitable, natural, totally understandable. And no matter how infuriated they get, they should never, the seminars tell them, never ever act as though we're not worthy. But what if we *aren't* worthy?

What do they do then? On this, the seminars are silent. *Figure that out for yourself,* the seminars seem to say.

Our babies start to cry; they start to struggle in our sweet babies' arms. They want to get down; they want to come to us. But our sweet babies won't let them.

"Jesus, what kind of person *are* you?" our sweet babies want to know.

We stop trying to put on our boots, and look at our sweet babies, wondering if they *really* want to know. Do they really want to know what the two protestors know: that we are the kind of people who, when interrogating someone, shove our rifles in his face and say, "If you don't tell us what we want to know, we are going to chop off your head and fuck your skull"? Do they want to know what the two protestors don't know? Do they want to know that we are also the kind of people who then, when it comes down to it, will not do what we've threatened? Except for Sanders, once, kind of. We say "kind of," because the woman was already dead. She was already dead. We had killed her while storming the house, or someone in the house had shot her beforehand, or during, or she had shot herself. In any case, she was dead, slumped against the wall. There was a small hole in her chest, and there was a lot of blood still coming out of it and staining her robes. She was wearing so many robes, so many layers of clothing, even though it was so hot; her headscarf had slipped down and was covering her face. We removed it. Her face looked like ash; she looked dead, but we put our hands inches from her mouth to feel if she was breathing; we put our fingers on her neck to see if she had a pulse. She wasn't and didn't; she was dead. Her son (we assumed he was her son; he was the right age, around ten or so) was still alive, facedown on the floor, hands behind his head. There was no one else in the house; we'd checked. We assumed we would do what we normally did: we would tell the boy who was still alive that if he didn't tell us what we wanted to know that we would cut off his head and fuck his skull. And then, when he didn't tell us, we'd bring him to the people who did the real interrogating, the people we knew nothing about, except that they used better threats than we did. Or they used the same threat, just more effectively. But before we could say what we usually said, Sanders blurted out, "If you don't tell me what I want to know, I'm going fuck your dead mother's skull." And then, before we could give him hell for deviating from the script, Sanders dropped his pants and tried to do what he'd threatened. Do our sweet babies want to know that? Do they want to know that when Sanders started to do it, we laughed? That all of us laughed? Maybe because we were so startled that he'd deviated from the script, or that he tried to do what he threatened. Or maybe because he kept saying, "It's not working, it's not working," and we said, "Well, *of course* it's not working, Sanders. She's dead." "That's not what I mean," Sanders said. "I'm talking about *it*. *It* isn't working." "Well, Jesus, Sanders," we said. "Of course *it* isn't working." And then we laughed; we couldn't help ourselves. Because Harold the protestor was right: it was kind of funny, if you thought about it. Do our sweet babies want to know that? Do they want to know that we are the kind of people who laugh at Sanders trying and failing to skull-fuck that dead mother? That we are the kind of people who laugh harder when Sanders, his pants still around his ankles, the *it* that wasn't working hanging out for anyone with eyes to see, waddles over to the son? The son is lying facedown on the dirt floor of his house—if it *is* his house, or if you can call it a house; it's just a stack of cinder blocks with planks of wood resting on top, really. The son is crying, the dirt getting wet around his head from his tears, his hands still clamped behind his head, keeping his head still while the rest of his body shakes and writhes and convulses, like a snake with its head nailed to the ground. "Look at me," Sanders, his rifle in his right hand, says to the son. He turns his head in Sanders's direction. "You're next," he says, cupping his crotch with his left hand, and we laugh harder. *That's* the kind of people we are.

But our sweet babies don't want to know this, any of this. So, instead, we say, "We are the kind of people, who when we get home, before we do anything else, put on our pointy boots and parade around the Public Square." And then, finally, we cram our round-toed boot feet into our pointy boots, and go do that.

IT IS HARD-SLEDDING getting to the Public Square. For one, it's snowing, again, again, and there is nowhere left to put the snow—the snowbanks are too high already—and so the walks are unshoveled, the roads unplowed. For another, our pointy boots have shit for traction and we slip and fall, a lot, as we walk. By the time we all get to the Public Square, we are soaked and sore from all the falling. Cold, too. Because all we have on is our travel camo pants and jackets, our berets, and, of course, our pointy boots, which are at least waterproof, and good thing, too, because they're completely buried in the snow. It is dark, after six o'clock. The county office building windows are dark; everyone has gone home. On the corner of State and Lewis, the bail bonds office has an illuminated Western Union sign in the window, but otherwise the place is dark, too. The guys in the halfway house are nowhere to be seen. It's possible that the halfway house has closed. It's possible that they've joined up, too, that the Army is where the halfway house guys are sent when a halfway house closes. The Bon-Ton is no longer the Bon-Ton, is no longer anything, but the city has decorated its front windows with white blinking Christmas lights. The streetlight poles are wrapped with green garlands and red bows. The statue of the Revolutionary War general is buried up to his waist in snow, the falling snow piling up on his plumed hat. Other than him, we are the only ones on the Square. It is not we how pictured it, not how we remembered it. For that matter, we're not sure how we pictured ourselves, how we remembered ourselves. We do a quick head count and find that we're not all here, not even close.

"Where the hell is everyone?" we ask. But we know. We

can see them putting the silver stars on top of their Christmas trees; we can see them holding their sweet babies real tight; we can hear their babies calling them by name, each and every one of them.

"Those bastards," one of us says.

"Those bitches," another one of us says.

"This is ridiculous," the third of us says.

"Maybe we should just go home," the fourth of us says.

"Our poor babies," the fifth of us says.

"Our poor sweet babies," the sixth of us says.

"Poor Sanders," the last of us says, and then we remember why we can't go home. His funeral is at nine in the morning. We can picture it: his sweet baby and baby will be there, trying to be brave, trying not to cry while the chaplain conveys the thanks of the president and prays to God for the state of Sanders's immortal soul. We'll be there, too, wearing our pointy boots. Because we promised Sanders, right before he died. He said, "When you lay me to rest, will you please wear your pointy boots?" We promised we would. But first, we need to do what we've come here to do. We have fifteen hours to parade around the Public Square in our pointy boots, fifteen hours to forget what happened to Sanders, so we can help bury him.

"Are we ready?" we ask each other. And then we start parading around the Public Square. We walk slowly at first, take tiny steps, because of the footing. But then we start going faster. We don't mean to. It's the blinking Christmas lights: they blink too fast, and when we look at them, they make us walk too fast, too. Right in front of the Bon-Ton, after only one lap around the Public Square, we slip, and fall on our backs, and because it's impossible not to laugh when someone slips and falls in the snow, we laugh. Then we remember laughing at Sanders and we stop laughing. Then we remember when we stopped laughing at Sanders and looked around. There was the mother, lying on the dirt floor, faceup, the way Sanders had left her. There was the son lying there, facedown and to the side, still weeping, still looking at Sanders, who was still grabbing his crotch with one hand and holding his rifle with the other. But Sanders wasn't looking at the son, or the mother, or at us. His eyes were closed, his face pinched in concentration. We knew what he was doing: he was trying to picture the day we'd paraded around the Public Square in our pointy boots; he was trying to replace the picture of what he'd just done with the picture of us, our boots, the Square, us parading around it, people watching us, us feeling so good. We knew that's what he was doing, because we did the same thing: we closed our eyes and tried to picture it, tried to remember it. We tried so hard. But the harder we tried to picture the boots, the Public Square, the office workers and bail bondsmen and halfway house guys, the farther away all of that was. All we could see was the mother, Sanders kneeling over her, us laughing; Sanders getting up and waddling over to the son, us laughing even harder. *Go away,* we told the memory we didn't want. *Please come back*, we told the one we did. *Please come back*, we begged our pointy boots. But they didn't.

We opened our eyes. Sanders was lying on the ground next to the son. They were both crying now—the son, because he didn't know what was going to happen, Sanders, because he did.

"I'm sorry," Sanders said.

"I am, too," each of us said.

"Will you promise me something?" Sanders said. "When you lay me to rest, will you please wear your pointy boots?"

"We will," we said, and then without saying another word, we aimed our guns at him, and one by one—Carson, Marocco, Smoot, Mayfair, Penfield, Rovazzo, Zyzk, Palmer, Reese, Appleton, Exley, Scarano, Loomis, Olearzyck—we shot him, and then we shot the son, too. Then we closed our eyes again. But we saw the same thing as before, except that there was another Sanders and another son, and they were both dead, and we'd killed them.

"Are you still seeing it?" we ask. But of course we know the answer. We lie there, in the snow, waiting to see whether one of us, any of us, will get up, brush off our pointy boots, and try again.

# The Misunderstandings

························································

**T**he misunderstandings started on a Wednesday, a not-so-unusual early February Wednesday when I was supposed to make dinner, but time had gotten away from me, somehow, again, even though I had so much of it—even so, it was already six o'clock and I hadn't yet introduced the pot to the burner, and the kids were staggering around and moaning theatrically about their big hunger. Katherine, our eight-year-old, was doing her best to distend her stomach, because at school her class had just finished a unit on People Less Fortunate Than Us, and so she knew all about the poor Somali children and their highly preventable famine, and she also had learned the Somali word for "please," and so she was lurching around with her little stomach as far out it could go saying, "Please, please," in the manner of a Somali kid who was starving to death—which is to say, pathetically, in a way that could either break your heart or step on your last nerve, depending on how many times your heart had already been broken and how hardened it had become—and as I turned around to ask Katherine if she knew the Somali words for "shut up," I accidentally struck my six-year-old son, Sam, in the head with the pot I was holding, and since the pot was filled with water, it had more heft than an empty pot, and I'll admit that it might have hurt some if it struck you, unexpectedly, in the side of the head and if you were a six-year-old boy with a low threshold for pain in the first place. Sam dropped immediately to the floor and started wailing—incomprehensibly at first, then making a little bit more sense with each wail, until I finally understood that he wanted to go to the hospital for stitches (there was a bump on the side of his head, a good-sized one, but no cut or blood; I checked) and Katherine was still moaning, "Please, please," in Somali, and into the middle of this depraved scene, after a long day at work, walked Sharon, my wife, and she took one look at us and said, "Jesus, let's just go out to eat."

We went. We went to a Mexican place, Tegucigalpa's, that had just opened up in the old train depot. We hadn't been there before, so we assumed it was in the main part of the depot—the lobby or the concourse—and that it was large. It wasn't; it was in the old barbershop and was much smaller than we'd imagined. I mean, it was really small: three booths along the east and west walls, and then two small tables at the north and south poles and then a bigger table in the middle. We sat at the bigger, middle table (it was the only one empty) and, logistically speaking, we were at the very center of the room, at the center of attention, if you will, as if we were on a theater-in-the-round, which might explain the first misunderstanding that then led to all the subsequent misunderstandings.

So it was small. It was also quiet. One of those hushed, intimate places. That's why people went there, it was clear, for the quiet and the intimacy. Even though the married owners, who were also the servers and cooks, were dressed in gaudy his-and-her matador outfits—even so, there was a dignity about the place, about the other diners, who were speaking softly, so softly, so that even if, say, a husband and wife were talking about how the husband had been fired and couldn't find another job and what a lazy bum he was and how the hell were they going to pay the mortgage, etc., etc., you wouldn't know it, because they were talking about it softly, under their breath, with dignity.

That's not the way Sharon talked about it. She asked the question loudly, shouting practically—"Did you look for a job today?"—although, to be fair, she had to raise her voice to be heard over the kids, who were really making a racket. Because they wanted to sit in a booth, not the table we were at. They were demanding to sit at the booth, and I was grateful for this at first, because I could ignore Sharon's question. I hadn't, in fact, looked for a job—not that day, nor the day before, and so on—so as to deal with the kids. I said, "There are people sitting in the booths. They were here first. Besides, this table is fine."

"But they have chips," Katherine whined (you know how they whine). "In the booths, they get chips."

It was true that the people in the booths had chips and we did not, and I was about to explain to Katherine that it had nothing to do with the booths qua booths, the booths were not blessed with chips while the tables went without, that everyone got them and that we had just sat down, after all, and we'd be getting our chips in due time. But before I could explain all this, Sam yelled, "Chips!" He really belted this out; for such a little kid, he could make an awful lot of noise, and the one time we tried to bring him to Saint Mary's for Christmas mass, he was yelling so loudly that no one could hear the pipe organ, and we never went back, which was fine, really, since we don't believe in God, which ended up being part of one of the subsequent misunderstandings.

But this was the first misunderstanding. Sam bellowed out, "Chips!" and everyone looked at us when he did so, but he persevered; he kept on shouting it—"Chips! Chips! *Chips!*" What kind of parents would let their kid do this in a small, intimate restaurant, you might want to know. Didn't we shush him? Of course we did. We shushed him over and over again. But it did no good. He kept yelling, and our shushing kept getting louder, until the shushing was like yelling itself, and had become part of our table's generally disruptive noise, and people were staring at us by now, except for those people who were trying to ignore us, which, I grant you, was probably a losing battle.

The chips came (the female owner brought them over, and I thanked her effusively, and she accepted the thanks, begrudgingly, and wouldn't meet my eyes and practically sprinted away from our table). The chips quieted the kids down some. The other diners stopped looking at us and went back to enjoying their meals, their private conversations. I was glad. For Tegucigalpa's sake. Because the train depot had been empty for years, and even though it was a lovely old-timey building with a mosaic on the ceiling and soaring arches and buttresses and good gleaming-white tiled floors—even so, the city had let it go absolutely to hell, in the postwar years, until it finally wised up and secured the necessary federal and state grants, redid the whole thing, and then began searching for businesses to rent out space in the refurbished station. Tegucigalpa's was the first one, and thus far the only one. Everyone wanted it to do well. Because there were so many empty buildings in our city, and you couldn't throw a stick without hitting an old elementary school with boarded-up windows or a decommissioned church or a house that was about to fall off its ruined foundation into the river, which was already heavily polluted, by the way, even though most of the paper mills and textile factories along it were closed and no longer actively polluting it. Yes, even if Tegucigalpa's succeeded, then the city still had a long way to go. Nearly everyone we knew had moved south or west, and the local economy was in awful shape; there were no jobs anywhere, and I tried to explain this to Sharon, but quietly, with some sense of decorum, and out of respect for the other diners.

"There are no jobs," I said. "I didn't look for jobs today because there aren't any."

"Oh, that's such garbage," she said. I knew what was coming next. I knew that she'd say that anyone who wanted a job could get one; after all, she'd gotten one, hadn't she? Even after not working for six years while she raised the kids and with not much experience and a worthless college degree (she'd been a religion major), hadn't she managed to get a job, a good job as a caseworker in the county office of social services?

"You got the job," I said, still quietly, but not as quietly as before, and if you were sitting at an adjacent table or the one adjacent to that, you might have heard me. "You got the job because your father got you the job."

"Steven, don't you dare," she said. "Don't you dare say that."

It's true; I shouldn't have said it. This is not something a husband should be saying to his wife, especially an unemployed husband. No, I shouldn't have said what I'd said, even if her father was a county commissioner, and even though she'd gotten the job without even submitting a regular application. But didn't she think it was odd that the county would hire someone as a social worker without any prior experience or educational background in social work? These are just some of the things I shouldn't have said but did.

"I am so sick of you," she said when I was done, and, boy,

was her face red; it always got fiery red when she was furious or embarrassed, and I used to find it lovely and endearing, although I didn't right then and hadn't in some time, come to think of it. "I'm so sick of your fat face."

"Hey," I said. "That's not fair," even though it's true that I had put on a few pounds out of depression since I'd been fired, which I thought was totally understandable, considering the circumstances. Although I tried not to consider the circumstances too often: because the circumstances were that I'd been fired—I'd been a history, sociology, civics, political science, and geography professor at the local community college—for having an affair with one of my students. My wife knew about this, of course, and had plenty to say on the matter, but that's more part of the second misunderstanding than the first, and I don't want to get ahead of myself.

A booth opened up—we clearly had driven the people away, because their enchiladas with mole sauce weren't even half-eaten—and the kids saw this and, with their mouths absolutely crammed with chips, they started chanting, "Booth! Booth!" except with their mouths so full, it sounded as though they were chanting "Oof! Oof!"

"We're not moving to any booth," I said. "So forget about it."

"I repeat," Sharon said, again raising her voice to be heard over the kids, who were still chanting, "Booth," but double-time and with more desperation. "Your . . . fat . . . face."

"Just everyone shut the fuck up!" As I screamed this—and I did scream it; there is no sense in arguing otherwise—the male owner of Tegucigalpa's loomed over me, over us, over our table, his arms across his chest, and clearly he meant business. Yes, he stood there like Judgment himself, and we all sucked in our breath, us and the other customers, and even the kids, who stopped chanting, although they were still cramming chips into their mouths, munch-munch-munching away while we waited to hear his verdict.

His verdict was laughter. He started laughing, first chuckling softly to himself and shaking his head and then really busting a gut, laughing nearly as loudly as the kids had been chanting, and his laughing was such a relief and so infectious that we started laughing, too, not knowing what we were laughing at, exactly, which somehow made the whole thing funnier (you know how it is), until all of us were wiping tears from our eyes and other diners were roaring and banging on the table and Sharon was flapping her hands in front of her face saying, "Oh, stop it, stop it. I can't stop laughing."

"Oh, that was good," the owner said, finally getting ahold of himself. "You really had me going for a second, didn't you?"

"We really did," I admitted, because even though I had no idea what he was talking about, the kids were laughing and Sharon was laughing and I was laughing, and we were happy, as a family, for the first time in god knows how long, and I didn't want to clear up this misunderstanding and put the kibosh on our happiness; not yet I didn't.

"I've heard about stuff like this," the owner said. "You're just terrific. Did Aaron at Salsa's put you up to this?"

"He did, he did," I said. This was a lie: Salsa's was a restaurant I knew all too well, but I had no idea who Aaron was, or what he'd supposedly put me up to.

"Oh, that son of a bitch," he said, and you could tell he was trying hard to not break into laughter again, and throughout the restaurant, people were calming themselves down, saying, "Hoo, hoo," like owls. "He really is a son of a bitch, isn't he?"

"He is," I said. "He really is."

"Listen," the owner said, "I want you to get back at him for me. I want you to do to him what you did here tonight. At Salsa's. Can you do that? I'll pay for your meal tonight and for your meal at Salsa's, plus another hundred dollars if you get back at him for me. Can you get back at him for me?" And so on and on until it became clear that he, the owner, assumed that our screaming and bad familial behavior had been part of a joke, some sort of prankish guerilla dinner theater paid for by a rival restaurateur. Sharon understood this, too, and was staring at me, as if to say: *Are you going to clear up this misunderstanding?* But her staring also had a knowing quality to it, as if to say, *You're not going to clear up this misunderstanding, are you?* No, I was not going to clear up this misunderstanding, not when it was going in my favor, which so many things recently had not. So I said, "Sure, sure. we'll get back at Aaron at Salsa's for you."

We did, the next Wednesday. Although the intervening week had been rough; I should say that. Because what, at first, had been merely a misunderstanding at Tegucigalpa's became, the more Sharon thought about it, a lie, which reminded her of the other lies I had told over the years. I tried to argue that a misunderstanding was not the same as a lie, in the same way that a cousin by marriage was not the same as a blood cousin, but she wouldn't have any of it. It was a lie all right, Sharon said, and it reminded her especially of my most recent, monstrous deceit, which was, of course, my affair with my student. And to make matters worse, during the course of that affair, I had taken my student and lover out to dinner at Salsa's many times, where I had used my credit card to pay for dinner, my credit card, which was also Sharon's credit card, which, along with some other missteps, was how I was eventually caught. In the week between our first misunderstanding and our second, Sharon really gave me the business over the affair, which had been over now for nearly a year. Even so, she had every right, and I didn't completely begrudge her the opportunity to remind me, again, what a louse I had been, and an awful husband and father and human being, and how lucky I was that she didn't dump my ass out on the street, with the rest of the bums.

But the one thing Sharon had never done was bring up my student-and-lover's race. She was black. Sharon knew this. But it hadn't come up, and I thought it was heartening—both as a husband and as a free-thinking progressive citizen of the world—that I was married to a woman who had such high principles that she could call her husband's young student mistress a whore, homewrecker, bimbo, slut, and so on, and never refer to her race in a disparaging way, and that maybe as a culture, we'd moved beyond such problems, and that maybe as a married couple, we could move beyond my interracial affair, too. So, no, Sharon had never raised the subject of my lover's race, and she didn't bring it up in the week between our first and second misunderstanding, either.

But it came up at Salsa's. Again, this was a Wednesday. To be true, I'd all but forgotten that we were there on Tegucigalpa's behalf, to get back at Aaron, whom I assumed was the owner of Salsa's. Because the owner of Tegucigalpa's had given us a gift certificate, and you know how easy it is, once you have the certificate, to forget who gave it to you and why. No, it was just another Wednesday, where I hadn't yet gotten dinner on the table and the kids were a mess and Sharon was tired and hungry after a long day at work and we needed something to eat, and so I said, "Let's go to Salsa's."

Sharon looked at me in shock, eyes bulging thyroidally and theatrically (her thyroid was fine), and said, slowly, making sure I understood: "Are you sure you want to go to Salsa's? Are you sure that's where you want to go for dinner?"

I know now, just as I knew then, why Sharon was asking this question. She was giving me a chance to change my mind, a chance to remember the awful week that had just passed, a week devoted to long, teary discussions of my crimes of passion and how it was possible that we'd never truly recover from them, and how some of these crimes of passion from which we might not ever truly recover took place at Salsa's, where I now wanted us to go to eat. I know this now, and I knew it then, too: but we were all so hungry, and I had been in the house all day and wanted to get out, and we had this gift certificate, and we weren't exactly rolling in money, because of my joblessness, which over the previous week had been a common topic of discussion, along with my affair. And speaking of my affair, it had been a year now, nearly, since it was over, and I figured, dammit, it was high time to forgive and forget, which is what people say when they've never had to forgive and forget anything or -one before.

In any case, I knew why Sharon was asking this question, but I pretended not to, and said, "We have a gift certificate."

"Are you sure you want to go to Salsa's?" she asked again, this time in stiff, threatening military fashion, as if to say *You do not want to go to Salsa's.*

"We have a gift certificate," I repeated.

"Are you sure you want to go Salsa's?" Sharon asked again, and this time there was a heartbreaking, begging quality to her voice, as if to say *Please don't make us go to Salsa's. If you love me, if you've ever loved me, you won't make us go to Salsa's.*

"We have a gift certificate," I said again: because apparently when you break someone's heart once, then it's almost impossible not to *keep* breaking that heart, and breaking it and breaking it, until it's completely broken and gone, and then you wonder how you could have ever fallen in love with a person so heartless.

"Fine," Sharon said, sighing in huge you-asked-for-it resignation. "We'll go to Salsa's."

So we went to Salsa's. I hadn't been there since Sharon had discovered my affair with my student, Torina, which was only a few days before the school discovered it and fired me, and only a few days after Torina herself dumped me. She had dumped me, in fact, at Salsa's, over a plate of tofu burritos. Salsa's was vegetarian, and since Salsa's was also environmentally conscious, they served tofu burritos without napkins, because of the vanishing trees and the rapacious paper industry and the diminishing ozone, and since Salsa's liked to think globally and act locally (it always said so on the chalkboard menu on the wall; they didn't pass out actual individual menus—again, because of the paper) they called their tofu burritos World Burritos, and a year earlier I was about halfway through my World Burrito when Torina dumped me.

Katherine and Sam were good this time; I have to say that. They didn't terrorize each other like they can do, and mostly they just sat there quietly, reading the books they brought with them while we waited for our food. All in all, they were model children, the kind of children you might admire if you were another diner at the restaurant and were yourself thinking about having children. Even I was admiring them—Sam's ruddy cherubic face and Katherine's long pigtailed black hair and smart black eyes—I mean, I was really scrutinizing them and so proud, and I wanted to stand up in the restaurant and shout *These beautiful children are mine. I made them.* But I didn't stand up and shout that, because, for one, it would have been seen as patriarchal, and Salsa's hated patriarchy, and, for another, I didn't want to draw any extra attention to myself. Salsa's was a college hangout, and on my way in I'd noticed Bob, who taught criminal justice, and Cheryl, who taught travel and tourism, and Lawrence who taught Portuguese, Spanish, French, and German. All of them, I knew, were looking at me, judging me, wondering how I could do what I had done with Torina—something so immoral and stupid and against college policy—and now my beautiful children were less something to be proud of and more condemnation, because how could I have done that to them, too?

I bet Sharon was wondering the same thing. She hadn't said anything other than to place her order—mostly she was sitting there staring at me, breaking her stare once in a while to shake her head, as if to clear it of something—and only when the food came did she break her silence. She said, "Do you still have the fever?" She said this in a voice that wasn't her voice, something meaner and higher than a hiss. "I bet you still have the fever, don't you?"

"What are you talking about?"

"Jungle fever," she said.

"Sharon!" I said, and I knew right then that I'd made a huge mistake, another one, and that we shouldn't have gone to Salsa's, gift certificate or no gift certificate. I'd never heard Sharon say anything remotely like that in our fifteen years together, and it was as if I were sitting across the table from someone else's wife, someone I didn't know and didn't want to know. I bet that's the way she felt, too, looking at the liar and cheater

I was, thinking that she knew me and didn't. And maybe this is what you do when you hurt the people you love—you turn them into something you don't love—because Sharon asked, loudly this time, like she didn't care who heard, "I bet she smelled different, didn't she? I bet she smelled like Africa. I bet she was a real black skank."

Everyone in the restaurant heard this, and their private conversations just about fell off a cliff. Even the cooks, waiters, and dishwashers stopped banging their Peruvian clay bowls and cups.

"What's a 'black skank'?" Katherine asked.

"Why don't you ask your father?" Sharon said. Her voice went back to normal for a second, and then she looked at me, pretty much lost it again, and said in a voice a snake might use if she were talking to another snake who was hard of hearing, "Why don't you ask your father what a 'black skank' is?"

"Dad," Katherine said—because she really is quite a student; her quarterly report cards can't say enough about her wide-ranging, inquisitive mind—"what's a 'black skank'?"

What do you say to a question like that? Maybe someone working in high-rise construction might have answered it one way; maybe someone in the radio business would have answered it in another. But I was a teacher, or had been, and when Katherine asked her question, my teacherly instincts kicked in. In fact, this was why Torina dumped me—I'd been talking about the origins of the tofu in her World Burrito, and she'd said, "You're always teaching me something I don't need to know," and then, "I don't think this is going to work"—but I tried not to think about Torina, and answered Katherine's question the best I could.

"A 'black skank,'" I said, "is a derogatory term for an African American woman. It's an incredibly offensive term, and you should never, ever use it. Not in public. Not in private, either."

"Oh," Katherine said, and went back to her book, which, I believe, was an Encyclopedia Brown, about how he found his neighbor's missing wallet.

But Sharon wasn't done. "Tell us about her booty, Steven," she said. "Tell us about her big lips on your *thang*. Was she happy with your *thang*? Was it smaller than what she was used to? Were you bling-bling enough for her?"

Katherine looked up from her Encyclopedia Brown again and said, "Dad . . ."

But I knew what she was going to ask, and so I said, "Your mother is using a number of racist stereotypes—mostly physical. For instance, that black women have big"—and here I struggled for the right way to put this—"*rear ends*, and big lips, and that black men have large . . ." And here again I struggled—who wouldn't have? "*Things*," I finally said.

"But Mom didn't say 'things,'" Sam said. "She said 'thang.'"

"That's right," I said, and truth be told I was proud of him, because—unlike his sister—Sam had never done particularly well in school, and, as his first-grade teacher had pointed out, he was never really particularly interested in *anything*, and that he'd noticed that his mother had said "thang" instead of "thing" was a real breakthrough. "Your mother said 'thang,' and she also said 'bling-bling.' Both are part of the African American lexicon, or at least we're led to believe that this is so by popular media. Truth be told, African Americans speak in lots of different ways, and it's important that we not essential-ize in any way."

"But why is Mom saying these things?" Katherine asked.

"Your mother is talking about a specific woman, sweetie," I said. I'd never told the kids about Torina. In fact, Sharon and I had agreed that we wouldn't, that it wasn't something they needed to know. But maybe it was. As any teacher knows, you sometimes don't know what needs to be taught until you teach it. "The woman she's talking about is African American."

"But why," Katherine asked, "is she saying all these bad things about the woman?"

"She's saying these bad things," I said, "because *I* did some bad things with the woman. The bad things have nothing to do with her being an African American, though. I think it's important to remember that."

"And are you sorry you did the bad things?" Katherine asked. Because if we've taught our kids nothing else, we've taught them all about being *sorry*. We've pretty much drilled it into their little heads that you have to admit to being *sorry* about the bad things you've done before you can go on and do something else for which you'll eventually have to apologize.

"Yes," I said, looking straight at Sharon, who was looking

down at the table and refusing to meet my eyes, for which I didn't blame her; I didn't. "I've never been so sorry about anything in my life."

"And is Mom sorry? For saying all those bad things?" At this, Sharon started crying, which I took to mean yes, she was sorry. I put my hand gently on her shoulder and said, "Please don't cry, I'm sorry, it's OK, it's all my fault, I love you, it's OK, you were right, we should have never come to Salsa's, I'm so sorry."

"I know, I know," she said. She wiped her face with the back of her sleeve—again, because there were no napkins—and then said, "I think I'm crying because I'm so hungry. Are you so hungry, too?"

I wasn't so hungry. I wanted to get out of Salsa's, pronto, because of the scene we'd just made and what my ex-colleagues might have to say about it—on top of the many other things they'd already said in the halls, in the student newspaper, and in the faculty meeting where I was fired. The restaurant was still graveyard quiet, and I wanted to get the hell out of there. But we are the accumulation of the debts we owe and the way we pay them, and if Sharon wanted to stay and eat, then we would stay and eat. I looked up to see if our food was on its way, and in doing so I could see the eyes of Bob, my ex-colleague, the criminal justicist. It was strange: Bob's eyes weren't full of recrimination and disgust, the way I thought they'd be. They were wet and soft, and this surprised me, and it also surprised me when Bob stood up and started clapping—slowly at first, then faster, and then other people stood up and joined him, and soon the whole restaurant was on its feet, giving us an ovation.

They were giving us a *standing* ovation, and this scared the kids a little. Sam climbed into his mother's lap, and Katherine hugged her Encyclopedia Brown book tight to her chest. Who could blame them? I was pretty unnerved by the whole thing, too—even more so when a large white man with an overgrown red beard and dreadlocks came over to our table, applauding as he walked toward us. This turned out to be Aaron, the owner of Salsa's, the "son of a bitch" the owner of Tegucigalpa's wanted us to get back at for him.

"I just wanted to tell you," Aaron said, "that was the bravest thing I've ever seen."

"It was?" I asked.

"It was," Aaron said. He told us that, as a member of Greenpeace, he'd confronted whaling ships in a tiny leaking dinghy; he told us that, as an Earth Firster, he'd chained himself to a nuclear reactor, or at least a fence surrounding it. "But I've never seen anything as brave as what you just did."

"Well," I said.

"I mean, it's easy to forget how racist we all are," Aaron said. And then he turned to face his customers and said, "*All* of us. You are *all* racist. Don't think you're not." The customers put their heads down when he said this, but they kept clapping, as if applauding their own racism.

"Well," I said again.

"Thank you for teaching us a valuable lesson," he said.

"You're welcome," I said. At this, Sharon started crying again. I thought she was still crying about Torina and about the racist things she had just said and how I'd driven her to say them, and so I reached over the table and put my hand on her arm and said, "It's OK, it's OK," but she started shaking her head. Sharon was still crying, but the crying was light, and I could see a smile breaking its way through the sobs. She was happy, or close to it, and I asked, "What is it? Why are you smiling? Is it because we've been misunderstood again?"

She wagged her index finger at me, as if to say *Yes, that's it. You've hit the nail right on the head.*

"Dad, it's like magic," Katherine said. She leaned across the table and put her hand next to mine on her mother's arm, and then Sam reached up (he was still sitting on Sharon's lap) and put his hand on her cheek, and there we were, the three of us, laying our hands on Sharon, and for a moment she was like the Blarney Stone without the kissing.

"What's like magic?" I asked Katherine.

"*We* are," Katherine said.

Aaron was still standing there, and clearly uncomfortable with this outpouring of family emotion, and so to avoid watching us, he kept turning back to his customers, as if to make sure they hadn't forgotten that they were racists. But soon, Sharon quit crying and we took our hands off of her, and Aaron sat down at our table and said, "I have a proposition for you."

I knew what was coming next. Sure enough, there was a

diner down the block—Mickey's, whose owner and customers were known for their rabidly conservative politics, and
Aaron wanted to us to teach them the kind of lesson we'd just
taught at Salsa's. So we went, the next week, and it happened
to be the same week we had to put my mother in the nursing
home, and so Mickey's customers (AARP members, one and
all) thought our argument about whether my mother would
survive through the New Year and whether we could afford it
if she did—thought it most timely and thought-provoking,
and they pledged to update their living wills, right away. Then
*they* hired us to go to the Friday fish fry at Saint Agnes's church
hall, except it wasn't at all clear what we were supposed to
do there.

Sam felt this lack of direction deeply and kept asking,
"What are we *doing* here?" When I couldn't give him a good
answer, he made a big, loud point of asking who the guy was
on the cross (there was a crucifix on the hall's south wall) and
I said, "That's Jesus," and Sam happened to be in a particularly foul mood that night and said that Jesus was "stupid,"
Jesus was "made up," Jesus was "ugly," and we kept shushing
him and saying, "Even so, even so," and the people at Saint
Agnes's thought this was a masterful sermon on the power of
blind faith, and so on and so on. And while we still had our
family problems, still couldn't forget the ways in which we'd
hurt each other and how our lives together hadn't worked out
the way they were supposed to—even so, as long as we were
being misunderstood, we were happy, happier than we'd been

in a long time. It was more than happy: we started feeling extraordinarily *blessed* in our misunderstandings, and we also ended up getting quite a reputation in our city, making an extra dollar or two, so much so that on our sixteenth wedding anniversary Sharon and I could afford a sitter for the kids and go to dinner at the Rio Bamba.

The Rio Bamba was the nicest restaurant in town—all low lighting and red, plush, well-upholstered chairs, and waiters dressed to the nines. It was the first time we'd been there, the first time in over a year that we'd been to a restaurant without the kids, and it was also the first time we hadn't been hired to go out to eat since we went to Tegucigalpa's two months earlier. Sharon looked lovely, and I told her so, and she thanked me, but other than that, we didn't seem to have much to talk about, and so we sat there in silence, and the silence became so deep and awful that I knew I had to say something, and so I told Sharon, "You look lovely."

"You already told me that," she said. And then: "We were married sixteen years ago tonight."

"That's true," I said.

"Do you remember what we promised each other that night?"

I did: they were the standard vows—that we would always love, honor, and cherish—and I recited them at our wedding, and I recited them at the Rio Bamba, too, without any problem.

"Did you mean what you said back then?" Sharon asked.

"I did," I told her. "I truly did."

"I did, too," she said. "But what about now? Can you say the same thing now?"

Oh, if there were ever a time when I needed a big public misunderstanding, then this was it. Because I knew the answer to Sharon's question, and the answer was: *No, I can't say I'll love you forever. I have no right to even* talk *about love, after what I've done to you; after what I've done to you, I'm not even sure what love is, anymore.* But these are not the kinds of things you say to your wife on your sixteenth wedding anniversary, and so I let my teacherly instincts take over again, turned the question around on her, and asked, "Can *you* say the same thing now?"

Sharon didn't say anything, and neither did I. We just sat there and stared at each other, stared long and hard, as people do when trying to understand each other for the very first time.

# That Which
# We Will Not Give

································································································

**O**n Thanksgiving, when the Murray family gathered at the house on Wasson Road, there was
always a time when—after the food had been
served and consumed; after the table had been cleared; after
the Murray women had washed the dishes, and the Murray
men had sat at the table and wondered as a group why they
had eaten, say, so much of the creamed onions when they
didn't even *like* creamed onions; after the Murray women had
returned to the table, taking off their yellow rubber gloves
(they wouldn't wash a dish without first snapping on a pair of
yellow rubber gloves) and, with their faces pinched, looking
very much like physicians just after conducting a particularly
unpleasant invasive exam; after each after-dinner proposal
(to have another drink, to play a board game, to go see a
movie, to take a walk, to do *something*) was made and then
rejected—then and only then would one of the children ask,

"Do you remember that Thanksgiving when Mom asked Dad for a divorce and he wouldn't give it to her?"

This was in Cincinnati, Ohio, on the east side of the city, in one of those formidable brick Victorian houses that you couldn't dynamite off its foundation and that had pocket doors long since removed, for fear, maybe, of something being hidden behind them, and gas instead of wood fireplaces, because of the inevitable termites in the wood or soot buildup in the chimney or inconsistency in the heat. It was Mr. and Mrs. Murray's house, the house in which their children, Dudley and Penelope (they were twins) and Winslow, had grown up. The Thanksgiving that Mrs. Murray had asked for a divorce and Mr. Murray refused to give her one, Penelope and Dudley were thirteen, and Winslow was five. That Thanksgiving, they'd eaten their meal, but Mrs. Murray and Penelope hadn't cleared the table, and the turkey carcass and the untouched watery cranberry roll and half-eaten pumpkin and apple pies were still there in front of them, as if in reminder of some unfinished business. Throughout the dinner, Mrs. Murray had, at regular intervals, asked her husband for a divorce, and each time he had said no. Mrs. Murray had been asking for a divorce and Mr. Murray had been refusing to give her one for months and months, and the children knew this, knew also that their mother almost always got what she wanted, and so they had begun to view their parents' divorce with a sense of grim inevitability, as if it were not a matter of *if* but *when*, which was why Dudley (he was always the impatient one and years later caused a big scene at the IGA by cursing at the cashier, who, Dudley claimed, was making the already-long line longer with her "fucking small talk") finally asked, "Dad, why don't you just give it to her?"

At this, Mr. Murray—who was always playing fiery Tybalt or bloody Coriolanus or one of the tortured Richards or Henrys in his community theater's production of this or that play by the Bard and, because of that, had a taste for bombast and a distaste for clarity—stood up, pushed back his chair, and shouted, "Because a divorce is that which I will not give!" Everyone laughed at this, even Mrs. Murray, even Mr. Murray, who was not a man who laughed at himself: they laughed and laughed, and when they were done laughing, they assumed their normal post-Thanksgiving roles and Mrs. Murray didn't ask for a divorce again, and indeed, divorce wasn't ever mentioned in the family except at Thanksgiving, when they told the story.

THE STORY COULD be different, depending upon who was telling it and which part of the story they chose to emphasize. Because, as mentioned, Mrs. Murray had been asking for a divorce and Mr. Murray had been refusing to give her one for months and months before that famous Thanksgiving dinner, and while Mr. Murray shouting, "Because a divorce is that which I will not give!" was the last word, the most definitive word, it was not the only word.

For instance, there was the time, about two months before

that Thanksgiving, when Mrs. Murray was asking Mr. Murray to give her that divorce and he refused, and this infuriated Mrs. Murray. And so she started throwing books at him, books that had been passed down in the family from generation to generation, heavy oversized clothbound books that no one had read and no one would ever read—*Memories of a Grand Duchess*, *The Recollections of a Yankee Whaler*, *The History of the Ohio River Valley Coal Mining and Transport in Pictures*. Mrs. Murray chased him from room to room, hurling these books at him as she ran, until she finally cornered him in the pantry, where Mr. Murray put his arms over his face and withstood the barrage until there were no more heavy books, only paperback romances that Mrs. Murray refused to throw at her husband.

"Why?" Penelope asked at this moment in the story. She was sixteen at this point. "Why wouldn't you throw the paperbacks at Dad?"

"Because they were too small," Mrs. Murray said. "Too soft. They wouldn't have convinced your father to give me *anything*. Besides"—and here there was always a happy look on Mrs. Murray's face—"I thought I might want to read *those* books again, and I didn't want to ruin them by bouncing them off your father's hard head." At that, Mrs. Murray walked to her husband's end of the table and rapped on his head with her knuckles, to prove just how hard it really was and how lucky her fragile Jacqueline Susanns and Danielle Steels were to not have been hurled at it.

Penelope liked this part of the story—not because of the

happy look on her mother's face as she knocked on her father's head, or that her father let her mother do it, with a smile that was so full of begrudgement that it couldn't really be called a smile, but because Penelope had never been much of a reader, couldn't remember the difference between a metaphor or simile, and in ninth grade had been demoted from the advanced to the regular English section at school, and this part of the story told her why and that the demotion needn't trouble her. The image of her mother throwing those books at her father to no effect at all must have told her something about the uselessness of literature that she already knew or suspected, and every time Penelope heard this part of the story she felt less bad that she hated to read and swore anew that whatever she did when she grew up, it would not require reading: no, she would not pick up a book again, not ever, but would instead become, say, a dental hygienist, because she herself had perfectly straight, startlingly white teeth and felt so sorry for people who didn't.

THE FAMOUS STORY once, early on, almost got Winslow into trouble. He was in the fourth grade, only nine years old, and his class was to take a trip to the Indian burial mounds north of the city, the sort of trip that requires irrefutable proof of parental permission and emergency phone numbers and such. Winslow had been to the mounds twice before, and his mind had already focused on what was beneath the mounds—the bones and spirits of the noble Shawnee, and if, as the rumor had it, you stomped hard enough on the mounds, the Shawnee underneath would rise up and tell you to stop—and so he didn't hear at first when his teacher asked for an emergency number, and so she had to ask it several times, and finally Winslow, unhappily pushing the ghosts of the Shawnee aside, shouted, "An emergency number is that which I will not give!"

This stopped the class: they as a group looked at him in confusion, and so he began to explain about that famous Thanksgiving, and what his mother had asked for and what his father refused to give and what he had shouted. His fellow students seemed satisfied by the explanation—already Winslow knew that if one was going to survive as a student that one had better be satisfied by any explanation, no matter what it was or who was giving it—and drifted back into their own Indian mound reveries, but his teacher, Mrs. Wolfson, wasn't so satisfied. Her face peeled back in dismay, and her nostrils—already piggish—flared into small cave openings, and suddenly she was more frightening than all the Shawnee mounds in southern Ohio, and Winslow said, "Aw, I was just kidding," and then to distract her, he gave a series of emergency numbers, all of them made up on the spot. Mrs. Wolfson seemed grateful for the distraction and dutifully took down the numbers and never asked again about his family story. But even so, Winslow had the distinct impression that there was something wrong with his family and their story, and vowed never to speak of it again, and he also vowed to act as though it were not his story, and not his family telling it every Thanksgiving, after dinner. As far as Winslow was concerned, for a few minutes on the fourth Thursday of November he would be among strangers, strangers who were telling a story that had nothing to do with him.

THEN THERE WAS the business with the ties. Before she'd started hurling books at her husband, Mrs. Murray had, for a month or so, worn his ties. Because Mr. Murray had a huge disdain—a physical revulsion, really—for women who wore ties, and refused to patronize restaurants where the waitresses donned them as part of their uniform, and once, during one of his plays—a modern interpretation of *As You Like It* in which Rosalind pretended to be a male bond analyst in a three-piece suit who has drinks after work at the Yale Club—the actress playing Rosalind adjusted and fiddled with her double Windsor knot so obsessively that Mr. Murray (he was playing the usurper, Duke Frederick, who, in the new version of the play, was one of the duplicitous higher-ups at Goldman Sachs) began making involuntary gagging noises and had to run off the stage in the middle of the third act.

"Was it because you thought she was a lesbian?" Dudley always asked at this point in the narrative. He was the type of boy, and then man, who asked questions and indeed conducted normal conversation as though he were an investigative journalist or a combative cross-examining lawyer. "Are you saying that you hate lesbians?"

"No, that's not the issue at all," Mr. Murray always said, but then he never did say what the issue was.

In any case, when Mr. Murray refused to give his wife the divorce she wanted, his wife started wearing his ties—the broad-striped old-school ties from the old school he never actually attended; the paisley power ties he wore to the monthly regional-manager meetings for First Bank of Ohio; the ancient-looking monochromatic wool ties that his Anglo-Saxon forefathers probably wore while herding sheep or shoveling peat or some such thing. This went on for two months. Mrs. Murray wore the ties everywhere—to her job as director of charity and giving at the Episcopal diocese, to restaurants and cocktail parties, even to bed—and Mr. Murray never said a word against the practice. It's true that he seemed to have lost his appetite and fifteen pounds over those two months, and it's also true that when his wife started wearing ties to bed, he stopped sleeping and in the morning you'd find him at the kitchen table, pouch-eyed and on his fifth cup of coffee, asking, "Who knows what time it is?" But still, he never spoke out against it or denied his wife access to his tie rack, and when she had worn the final, rattiest frayed tie in the collection, she began throwing books at him instead and never wore his ties again, and for that matter, it had been years and years since he had even seen her wear a shirt with a collar. When Mr. Murray pointed this out, in the years after the famous Thanksgiving dinner, Mrs. Murray would once again rise from her chair and go to her husband's end of the table and they would make a big mock wrestling match out of her trying to yank off his tie (all the Murray men wore ties to Thanksgiving dinner, even when they were Murray boys) and him trying to prevent her, and this, of course, made everyone laugh, too.

DESPITE BEING BOMBARDED with books and terrorized by neckties, Mr. Murray became quite fond of the story, and found, after several Thanksgivings had gone by after the first one, that he could not help taking the lead in telling it, the same way some men can't help telling the story of how they survived the Bataan Death March or why they stopped voting in presidential elections or how they nearly became the first man to invent, copyright, can, and mass-market the baked bean. In his telling, Mr. Murray omitted the ties and books, and began simply by telling everyone how much he had loved Mrs. Murray from the first time he saw her, how beautiful she was in her wedding dress, how he was so lucky to be married to her (at this point in the narrative, Mrs. Winslow smiled at her husband, then excused herself and left the dining room), and then skipped right to the part where Dudley had asked, "Dad, why don't you just give it to her?" and Mr. Murray had responded, "Because a divorce is that which I will not give!"

Mr. Murray would then notice that Winslow had fallen fast asleep, head down on the table and drooling. For him, his father shouting "Because a divorce . . ." seemed more like an alarm clock than a call to arms. And not a very effective alarm clock, either, because Winslow stirred and moaned, but didn't awake: it was as though he heard his father faintly, from a great distance, as if it were part of someone else's dream calling to his own. No, the thing that always woke Winslow was not his father shouting what he shouted, but his brother slapping him hard in the back of the head and saying, "Wake up," and then slapping him again.

It should be said that while Winslow's nickname was Win, his brother's nickname was Dud, and Dud had always resented Win because of it. But the story of brotherly antagonism is familiar and overlong; we won't lengthen it here, except to say that the boys fought, and Penelope tried to bring peace to the table, and Mr. Murray sighed through his nose and regarded Winslow sadly. He had no worries about Dud, his older son, who listened closely and carefully to the story no matter how many times he'd already heard it, and who even chanted the famous words along with his father when the time came. No, Dud would be just fine. It was Win—skinny, distracted, sleepy, *bored*—that Mr. Murray was worried about. Clearly, this story didn't mean to his younger son what it meant to the father himself, the way a baked bean might be a diamond to the almost baked-bean baron, but just a baked bean to his almost baked-bean heir.

And what did his story mean to Mrs. Murray? It was difficult to say, for whenever he took the lead in telling it, his wife eventually left the table during its telling. Mr. Murray noticed this. There were plenty of things he was supposed to notice but didn't—he was completely blind to nature, for instance, and paid no attention to the pink flaring sunset, had no ear for the different sounds different birds make, and could never tell what makes poison oak not poison ivy—but Mr. Murray *did* notice that his wife was never in the dining room when he told his version of the story and shouted his motto, and that she reappeared only when the story was through, after Dud had smacked Win on the back of the head and Win had smacked back and Penelope had ultimately brokered a truce. Only then did Mrs. Murray emerge from the kitchen, blinking, as if coming out of a cave and into the light. "It's getting late," she would say. She had turned into the kind of woman who always reminded one of the lateness of the hour; Mr. Murray had noticed that, too, and he also noticed that she was much concerned with the cleanliness of public bathrooms (whenever they would go out—to dinner, the theater, a baseball game—Mrs. Murray would return from the bathroom and announce to her husband, "The ladies' room is quite clean"). The only time Mrs. Murray *wasn't* this kind of woman was when a Murray other than Mr. Murray was telling the famous story. Only then was Mrs. Murray the woman he wanted to remember—beautiful, happy, content. Mr. Murray loved telling the story—it was true; but he loved his wife even more than telling the story, and so he would give it up for her. *I will do that for you*, he almost told her, right there at the table, but she looked him straight in the eye and repeated, "It's getting late," and so he didn't.

WHEN PENELOPE GRADUATED from high school, as she'd promised herself, she read no more and went, instead, to dental hygienist school. The school was in Provo, Utah. Why she should go to Utah instead of staying in Ohio to learn to be a dental hygienist bothered her parents, for reasons that remained mysterious to them. It wasn't that they were against their children traveling, or that they were against their only daughter going so far away to school; perhaps it was that they were against Utah. But in any case, Penelope pointed out that it was no more expensive to go to dental hygienist school in Utah than it was in Ohio, and besides, she'd never been to Utah before, and wasn't this a good, practical excuse to go to somewhere you'd never been before? Mr. and Mrs. Murray had no adequate response to this, and so they let her go. And when, over her first Thanksgiving in Utah, Penelope said she wasn't coming home because she wanted to go skiing, they had no adequate response to that, either, except to say "We'll miss you," which she knew, and "You could always go skiing after Thanksgiving," which she also knew. But she went skiing over Thanksgiving anyway.

Unlike his twin sister, Dudley had enrolled at Ohio State, and unlike her, he did come home for Thanksgiving. He'd been at college for only three months, but already higher education had helped him aggressively develop his worst qualities. For instance, he had always had the thickest neck in his family, but he'd taken up weight lifting at the university and his neck had grown exponentially. It didn't help that he wore nothing but turtlenecks, turtlenecks with no sweater or shirt on top, and each turtleneck was so tight over his new muscles that he resembled a superhero out of the pages of L.L.Bean.

And then there was his new approach to the famous Thanksgiving story. Dudley had always felt the story deeply and couldn't understand why Winslow didn't seem to feel the same way. He often slapped his younger brother when he fell asleep at the table; that much has been told. But to be true, Dudley had always wanted to do something much more severe and permanent than slapping, something more along the lines of bone marrow surgery, in which Winslow would be opened up and forcibly given something he needed to have, whether he wanted it or not.

Thanksgiving dinner that year was quiet, tense, as though the Murrays were all waiting for some person or thing to take the place of Penelope. No one paid much attention to the food itself except to say that it was very good and that it made them very full. Mrs. Murray cleared the table by herself, and when she returned to the table from her dishwashing, Dudley immediately, without preamble, launched into the famous story. Except it wasn't the story, wasn't a version or an aspect of the story, but was instead an explication of the lessons to be learned from the story. Dudley had joined a fraternity at OSU, and he had also become a history and political science double major, and so he was much concerned with brotherhood and legacy and blood and the History of Man. "I've been thinking about it," he told them, and this was what he had been thinking: If you were a Murray man, he told them, then you could not give your wife the divorce she wanted, no matter how badly she wanted one. This was what the Murray men should take pride in, the yardstick by which they should measure themselves as Murrays. The Rockefeller men could all make money and find just the right charitable trust to hide it in; the Medicis could be counted on to rule benevolently and patronize the arts; the Kennedys had their full heads of hair and their overlarge teeth and libidos, and their in-the-prime-of-their-life assassinations and tragic airplane, automobile, and playing-football-while-downhill-skiing crashes. "And a Murray man," Dudley said, raising his voice just like his theatrical father, "will not give his wife the divorce she wants, no matter what."

They sat there in stunned, queasy silence. Dudley realized immediately that he had ruined both Thanksgiving and the story, which was the exact opposite of what he wanted to do. He loved Thanksgiving and the story very, very much, and now he had ruined them, these things that he loved, and how could one do that? He felt like crying or apologizing, except he had never done either of those things and had no confidence that he could do so now even if he wanted to, and instead he reached over and ruffled Winslow's hair. But even that gesture—which he'd meant to be fond and instead was violent—he misjudged, wrenching Winslow's neck in the bargain. He tried one last time to regroup and said, his voice full of mock threat, to Winslow, "When you get married, buddy, you can't give her a divorce, no matter what. Understand?"

"Whatever," Winslow said miserably, still rubbing his neck. He was eleven, after all, and as far away from marriage as Cincinnati was from Provo.

"What do you mean, 'Whatever'?" Dudley said, the anger pouring into his voice as the contrition poured out.

"Who wants some tea?" Mrs. Murray said, and then got up to go to the kitchen before anyone said that they did, or didn't.

The table was quiet for a minute. Finally, Mr. Murray began asking Dudley questions about the university (he had gone there as well and was much concerned about whether they still taught freshmen the fight song), and after enduring a few minutes of this, Winslow followed his mother into the kitchen. He found her standing at the butcher's block, her back to him. She was chopping at something with a knife (he couldn't see the knife, but there is no sound like a sharp, well-balanced knife on a butcher's block), slowly and deliberately chopping, and each time she did so Winslow could hear his mother suck in a painful, sharp breath, and because of that and because Winslow couldn't see the hand that wasn't doing the chopping, either, he had the distinct impression that his mother was chopping off her own fingers, one by one.

Of course, Mrs. Murray was probably just chopping lemon for the tea and in any case, still has all her digits. But the point is, Winslow knew something was wrong, and despite his vow years earlier to detach himself from his family and their story on this night, he was nonetheless having thoughts about his family and maybe the world of families being full of barbaric rituals and traditions designed to leave our humanity behind, rather than enlarge it. Winslow could have asked questions, about the whys of his mother's crying and maybe even about the hows of preventing his own future wife having at her digits with her own knife. He could have at least gone over and comforted his mother, or tried to. But he didn't. He didn't. You couldn't comfort your mother and pretend that she wasn't your mother at the same time. Instead, Winslow quietly backed out of the kitchen and into the dining room, with the rest of the Murray men, where, apparently, he belonged.

PENELOPE DIDN'T COME home next Thanksgiving, either, but there was another woman there for dinner. Her name was Susan; she was Dudley's new girlfriend. Like Dudley, everything about Susan was big: her head of hair was big and piled high, her laugh was big and throaty, and she was nearly six feet tall and walked with a slight limp from a high school volleyball injury. Susan was more than a match for Dudley: she seemed to be able to deflate him without humiliating him, and the Murrays were all grateful for this. In truth, Dudley seemed grateful for it as well: perhaps he feared what would happen to him, or to someone else, if he weren't deflated.

The only other thing notable about Susan was that she was from Fort Wayne, Indiana, and spoke about Fort Wayne as if it were some faraway exotic land with its own customs and rituals. "In Fort Wayne," she told Mrs. Murray, "we make the stuffing *inside* the turkey." "In Fort Wayne," she said, "it doesn't usually snow on Thanksgiving, but when it does, it's very pretty." And so on.

The first year Susan was with them, Mrs. Murray—as though in Susan's honor—told the most outlandish of the stories in their repertoire. This was after both the books and the ties, about a month before the famous Thanksgiving dinner, and once again Mr. Murray refused to give Mrs. Murray the divorce she wanted, and this of course infuriated Mrs. Murray, and so she began doing things designed to embarrass her husband in front of their neighbors. She did tai chi on the lawn, in her pajamas, every morning at dawn; during full moons or waxing moons or gibbous moons or pretty much any sort of moon, she dressed in dark robes decorated with symbols of the occult, the way a Wiccan might, and howled at the moon, howled and howled, until the neighborhood dogs all joined her in chorus; months in advance of Christmas, she bought or built elaborate, oversized illuminated snowmen, reindeer, Santas, cherubim, baby Jesuses, adult Jesuses, black African Jesuses, Marys, Josephs, mangers, and wise men, and put them on the front lawn, the roof of their house and garage, and dangling from the flagpole—all in violation of strict neighborhood association codes. But Mr. Murray endured it, endured his neighbors' withering looks, endured the warnings and second warnings of the neighborhood association's executive board, endured this all quietly, so quietly, until finally she'd exhausted this particular grab bag of eccentricities.

"You didn't really howl," Winslow said, as he always did,

because he had no memory of the howling, aside from the story itself; it was the only time he ever spoke up, ever participated in the Thanksgiving storytelling. He hated himself for it; each time, he would steel himself to *not* say "You didn't really howl." And each time, it came out of his mouth anyway. It was inexplicable.

"I did," his mother said, and then, to prove it, began to howl right there at the dinner table. In the past, whenever she howled, Dudley was sure to join in. But Dudley didn't join in. Mrs. Murray stopped howling and turned to Dudley, who was staring straight ahead, as though there were a particularly infuriating and terrifying stain on the wallpaper. His family knew why: Susan. How had they not realized how odd this story might seem to her? What would she think? Would it drive her away from them, and from Dudley? And if so, would they be stuck with an even more militant version of Dudley? They all leaned toward Susan in anticipation, as if waiting for the jury to render its verdict, for the judge to hand down his sentence.

"Your neighbors must have thought you were a bunch of kooks," Susan said. "Now, in Fort Wayne . . ."

MR. MURRAY DIDN'T care whether his neighbors thought they were a bunch of kooks or not, and he certainly hadn't cared back when his wife was lobbying for divorce and he was denying her. Because back then, the Murrays' neighborhood had become an absolute incubator for divorce; there was no better advertisement for the moving industry than their block, and the block next to theirs, and the block next to that one. Every day there were new refugees out on the sidewalk, surrounded by their belongings, waiting for the moving van to take them and theirs away to their place of exile. One day there was Dr. Whitney and his medical books and his framed degrees and his leather chair and his full-sized skeleton that his children had given him as a joke birthday present; the next day there was Mrs. Huggins and her two moon-faced girls in their identical corduroy jumpers, surrounded by their unbunked bunk beds and serving buffets and antique dressers and boxes and boxes of their suddenly outdated framed family pictures and photo albums.

And there was Mr. Murray, on his front steps, the day after Mrs. Murray had ceased her howling. He could hear his children out in the backyard, playing a complicated game involving an old tennis ball, the side of their garage, and Winslow's dress shoes as rackets. Mrs. Murray was upstairs in their bedroom crying. She was crying, but at least she was not howling, and at least he hadn't given her the divorce, and at least their house was still their house, their clan still a clan. You couldn't say the same of Dr. Whitney, out there on the sidewalk with his few belongings, the totems of his new bachelorhood; you couldn't say the same of the fractured Huggins family and their sorry furniture. Mrs. Murray was upstairs crying—you could hear the arrhythmic sobs coming from the open window—but Mr. Murray was able to tune out the sobbing and the reasons for the sobbing. Because there were his sorry divorced neighbors on display, and Mr. Murray could point to them and say, *That is not me. That is not us. That is not me.*

PENELOPE SPENT THE next Thanksgiving in Provo, but finally, on her fourth year away, she came home for the holiday. She was snow-bunny tan and tooth white and generically beautiful in the way Mrs. Murray was in her husband's stories of when they'd first met. The Murrays had all assumed Utah would have effected some large change on her—deleterious, more likely than not—but that wasn't the case. No, the only change was that Penelope was constantly bringing her dental training into conversational play. She chided her mother for drinking too much coffee, because of the way it would certainly and permanently stain her teeth; she asked Winslow, who was a pen chewer, if he knew what that would do to a person's enamel. And speaking of enamel, Penelope was much taken with its hardness. "Do you know how hard enamel is?" she asked after Thanksgiving dinner. No one did. "It's harder than Daddy's hard head," and then she went over and knocked on it, which led to a retelling of the time Mrs. Murray had thrown books at her husband.

Susan was there at this Thanksgiving as well, and had come prepared with tales of her own family's eccentricity. Once the book-throwing story had run its course, she told the Murrays about the Desmonds (that was her last name) of Fort Wayne. There was her uncle's family who threw Christmas parties during which, at some prearranged moment, each family member (there were six) would form a line, pluck the stem off a cherry, place the stems in their mouths, and somehow tie the stems into knots, which they would then hold out in front of them—*ta-da!*—until the guests gave them and their nimble tongues due applause. Her other uncle's family would every Sunday make a midafternoon meal consisting of French toast and bacon, which they called, for obscure reasons, Monkey Night. And her own family would, at weddings or funerals or family reunions, fire off cannons, miniature cannons with miniature cannonballs, which tore through neighboring clothesline sheets and porch flags and, on occasion, bay windows.

"I don't believe it," Penelope said. She had the normal sisterly resistance to her brother's girlfriend, and she also had some resentment over the story itself, which seemed to Penelope not at all in the spirit of their normal story, which was not at all about eccentricity. What it was about, Penelope couldn't exactly say, but it certainly wasn't a story about a cannon, a tiny cannon with its tiny cannonballs; and this certainly wasn't the time to tell such a story; and Fort Wayne Susan certainly wasn't the person to tell it the way she was telling it, either, telling like a member of the family, like a substitute member of the family who had taken the place of a *genuine* member of the family in (it was now obvious) her too-long absence. "I don't believe it," Penelope said again.

"You don't believe what?" Susan asked.

"That you fire cannons," Penelope said. "In your neighborhood. Through your neighbors' windows."

"Not on purpose we don't," Susan said.

"I don't believe you even did it accidentally," Penelope said. "You'd get sued."

"Not in Fort Wayne you wouldn't." It wasn't Susan who said this, but Dudley. Penelope looked at her twin brother, dumbfounded, for a good thirty seconds. In truth, she had never particularly cared for him one way or the other, except as a twin brother for whom she was required to care. But now that it was clear that he was more Susan's than his sister's, Penelope loved Dudley beyond requirement, loved him the way their shared gestation suggested she should have always loved him. "I'm sorry," Penelope said, to no one in particular, then excused herself.

Susan began to get up to follow her, but then didn't. She didn't seem to know what to do with her hands, clasping them above the table as if in prayer, then fiddling with a napkin, and finally dropping them into her lap. Susan stared at her hands sadly, as if they had just disappointed her.

"What just happened?" Dudley asked. "What did I say?"

His brother and parents didn't answer. They regarded Dudley half-wistfully, and with a great collective distance in their eyes, as if the table were a ship and Dudley were leaning over the railing, waving his goodbyes.

EXCEPT DUDLEY DIDN'T say goodbye and never would. The next Thanksgiving was peaceful—Susan didn't mention her family traditions or Fort Wayne, and Penelope complimented her on her smile, and Susan said that she'd never even had braces as a child, and the two of them expressed their reservations about orthodontia as a practice and orthodontists as practitioners—and by the next Thanksgiving, Susan and Dudley were engaged to be married. Dudley announced that he had a job waiting for him at Procter & Gamble after graduation, and so, as a married couple, they would settle in Cincinnati, in the same neighborhood. The dinner was more celebratory than normal: Mr. Murray was triumphant and oratorical (he was in rehearsal to play Abraham Lincoln in a one-man play called *Abraham Lincoln*, and as such, he often spoke as though he were addressing the nation) as he praised his wife and her beauty and proclaimed, "Because a divorce is that which I will not give!" in a way that suggested such moments were inevitable and easily overcome in an otherwise long and happy married life. Mrs. Murray grimaced her way through this story but at least didn't get up from her seat during its telling, and Winslow actually let slip some of his detachment and gave his brother a half hug in congratulations. But the good feeling was short-lived; when Dudley asked him to be his best man, Winslow said, "That is an excellent idea," and then the two of them argued over what *that* was supposed to mean, exactly.

Meanwhile, the women were in the kitchen. They opened another bottle of wine, and while they drank it, Susan asked, "I'm curious . . ." and here she paused, and Penelope feared she was going to call Mrs. Murray "Mom," but she didn't. "Mrs.

Murray," Susan said, "why did you want that divorce so badly, anyway?"

"Because I noticed one day that he looked exactly like Warren G. Harding," Mrs. Murray said, without hesitation, "and I didn't think I wanted to be married to a man who looked like Warren G. Harding."

Penelope laughed: she could see Mr. Murray through the doorway between the kitchen and the dining room, and he did look exactly like Warren G. Harding (whom she had learned all about in grade school, along with the other Ohioan presidents). She laughed and laughed and laughed and couldn't stop, and her laughter then took on a disturbing, breathless quality that was closer to weeping than laughing, and then she stopped laughing altogether and started crying, right there in the kitchen, into her glass of wine. Because Penelope realized that she had never asked her mother why she had wanted to divorce her father, or why her mother had needed her father to give it her a divorce, why she didn't just go out and get the divorce without her father's permission; she was twenty-five years old, and it had never once occurred to her to ask these questions. What kind of daughter had she been all these years? And what kind of daughter was she now? Because she *still* didn't want to know why her mother had wanted what she wanted. She did not want to know, and if her mother started to tell her she would run right out the door and get on the next plane to Provo and never come back. No, all Penelope wanted was to cry, to cry and her mother to hug her and not ask why she was crying. Which is exactly what Mrs. Murray did.

As for Susan, she had no idea who Warren G. Harding was, or why he might make her slightly tetched future sister-in-law laugh, then cry. But she did know that her husband looked like a younger version of Mr. Murray, and if Mr. Murray looked exactly like Warren G. Harding, then so would her Dudley, and what, exactly, was so funny or sad about that?

IT SHOULD BE said that Winslow and Dudley never wondered why their mother wanted a divorce, either. Like Penelope, they remembered those long-ago months when their mother threw those books and wore those ties and howled that howl, and of course that had scared them, and of course they were happier once she stopped doing those things and instead told stories about them once a year. Because the more often the stories were told, the less often the children remembered that there might be anything behind the stories, until finally they were just stories, stories they told and listened to once a year, and that was all. And what was wrong with that? Was it so awful that they never asked why the divorces were being requested, and why they weren't given? After all, why the *monkey* in Monkey Night? What genetic map gives a family such talented tongues, and on what occasion did they first discover such talent? What is the history behind the cannons, and where, oh where, does one get the miniature balls to fire from them? If we asked and answered such questions about our families, would we still want them to be our families? If we asked and answered such questions, would our families even *allow* us to be in the family anymore? And if we weren't in a family anymore, then in what would we be?

AFTER CRYING IN her mother's arms, Penelope decided that she'd been away long enough. She moved back to Cincinnati, took a job in a large dental practice, and married Tim Walley, the oldest, most placid dentist there, the one who was never perturbed by his patients—not by their excessive bleeding or screaming, or their stubborn tartar buildup, or their lack or insurance coverage, or anything. Like Susan, Tim didn't seem at all bothered by the family's famous story, and Mr. and Mrs. Murray were grateful for him, grateful that he had rescued their daughter from being one of those blandly pretty women who never marry and people can never understand why. As they got older, Mr. and Mrs. Murray confused their chronology and often thought of Tim as the heroic dentist who had brought their Penelope back from Utah, and not just the dentist who happened to hire and then marry her back here in Cincinnati. When Tim was unable to answer their questions about what Provo was like, they thought he was just trying to spare them the details of their daughter's sad, lonely Utah life. They were grateful for that, too.

And then there was Winslow, who became the black sheep the Murrays had always known he'd become. After high school and college (first Ohio State, then a series of lesser state schools, until finally graduating from the least of them), he grew several beards and shaved them; rented a thousand apartments and lost a thousand security deposits; wrecked one car while driving sober and none while not; and failed the Ohio public education certification test by a wide margin, then passed it, just barely, before deciding not to search for a job that might require such certification. Instead, he moved—to New Jersey, Montana, New Mexico, Massachusetts, Michigan, then New Jersey again. He always came home for Thanksgiving—not so much because he loved and missed the family, but because he wasn't sure he wanted to be totally without one—and each time he went back to whatever state in which he resided at the time, the Murrays wondered if he would return for the next Thanksgiving. But Winslow always came back.

He always came back alone, until one Thanksgiving, when he was twenty-eight, he came back with a woman whom he had married, married without the Murrays knowing a thing about it. Her name was Ilsa. She was beautiful, and the Murrays, once they got over the surprise of her existence as their daughter- and sister-in-law, recognized that: she had lovely jet-black hair, and feet pointing slightly out, as if she had once been a dancer. Ilsa was friendly enough, too: she laughed when laughter was called for, and listened to the famous story without undue participation or judgment. But there was something about her that made the family uneasy. For one, Winslow, who had always been so private and detached, began to tell them things about Ilsa that he shouldn't, things they didn't much want to hear: the way Ilsa shaved her shins but not her thighs, and how soft that thigh hair felt when he ran his fingers over it; about the state-shaped moles (South Carolina, Rhode Island, and Oklahoma) on her back, and the precancer therein that the doctor had warned her to be vigilant about; the way her left armpit sweated when she was nervous, but not, mysteriously, the right one.

And then there was her name. The Murrays didn't know much about Winslow, but they did know that he was perverse, and they wondered whether Winslow would have fallen for her the way he had if Ilsa's last name had matched her first—if it were Johansson or Bergman or some such obviously Swedish surname. But Ilsa's last name wasn't Johansson; it was Zilkowski, Ilsa Zilkowski. And when Winslow told them that he loved her very, very much, they wondered if that didn't have something to do with the perversity of her name.

Finally, there was the matter of divorce. Ilsa was from a family of divorce: there were more divorces than not in her family, and her parents themselves had been divorced and remarried and divorced so many times that occasionally Ilsa had difficulty remembering who her biological parents were. She seemed amazed, after hearing the famous story, that no one in their family had ever been divorced. "Tell me the truth," Ilsa said. "Not anyone?"

They assured her that no one ever had.

"How is that possible?" Ilsa wanted to know.

This seemed to them an ominous question, and when Ilsa and Winslow returned to Jersey City, where they had met, gotten married, and now lived, Dudley predicted, "They'll be divorced in a year, tops." No one disagreed with him.

But he and they were wrong. Winslow and Ilsa returned the next Thanksgiving, full of news: they were going to move to Cincinnati, and Winslow was going to put his state certification to use and get a job teaching high school English, and they were going to start a family. In fact, they had already started one: Ilsa was pregnant.

"But why?" Mrs. Murray asked them. "Why are you going to move here?"

"Because we want to be around family," Winslow said. This was somewhat true: *Ilsa* wanted to be around family, and he loved her and wanted to give her what she wanted. Winslow was lucky enough to have a family he could give her.

"I've never really had a family before," Ilsa explained.

What could you say to something like that if you were a Murray? They all knew how the rest of the night would go. After Thanksgiving dinner, they would tell an especially long, complicated version of their famous story in honor of their prodigal brother and son and his pregnant wife, and at the end of their famous story they would rise as one and shout out, "Because a divorce is that which I will not give!" as if shouting it for all Thanksgivings past, and all Thanksgivings yet to come. Then Mrs. Murray would say, "It's getting late," and they would go upstairs to bed and count their blessings, as happy-and-whole families always do, thankful that they, like all families, had weathered some tough times, and that they, unlike most families, had their famous family story to help them weather, to help them forget, that which they had to weather. While they were upstairs, counting their blessings, Mrs. Murray would stay downstairs under the pretense of tidying up. Then, when she was certain that everyone had fallen asleep, Mrs. Murray would do what she always did, what she did on all Thanksgivings past and would do on all Thanksgivings yet to come: she would sneak into each bedroom and kiss each member of her brood—her husband, her children, and her children-in-law—gently on the forehead, then back out of the room and close the door behind her, as if she were saying her farewells, as if this were her last Thanksgiving and next year the family would tell a different story, a story about the Thanksgiving that Mrs. Murray had sneaked out in the middle of the night and left the Murrays and their marriages behind.

# Cartoons

......................................................................

**I** ran into my ex-wife outside the community center. I
mean this literally. I saw her before she saw me and then
pretended I hadn't seen her at all and knocked right
into her, and the manila envelope she'd been holding fell to
the ground, and then I picked it up and handed it back to
her, making a big gentlemanly deal about the whole thing. It'd
been eight years since we'd been married for twenty-two years,
and I still hadn't totally gotten over it yet.

"I always thought we'd grow old together," I said.

"We did," she said. "And now we're growing even older with
other people."

It wounded me to hear her say this. Although of course it
was true. By now we were remarried, to Allison and Robert,
both good people, people with whom we were friends during
our former life as a married couple. But whenever I saw my
ex-wife, I couldn't even remember their names.

"How's Allison?" my ex-wife asked.

"What's in the envelope?" I asked back.

"A cartoon," she said. "I'm taking a cartoon-drawing class at the community center."

"Hey, I did that," I said. It was right after we'd divorced, when I was willing to do anything to forget everything, no matter how dull it was, no matter how bad I was at it. These were the cartoons I tended to draw: cartoons of people stuck in bad weather and making the best of it; birds kibitzing at the bird feeder; men coveting each other's automobiles. The last cartoon I ever drew was of a group of men standing in front of a row of identical luxury vehicles, one man saying to the another, "I like yours better than mine, Don."

"It's really good," everyone else in the class had said. "I think you should send it to the *New Yorker*."

"I think I will," I said.

We always told each other that our cartoons were really good, and that we should send them to the *New Yorker*. And we always said that we thought we would. But we never did.

"Can I see?" I asked my ex-wife, and then grabbed the envelope out of her hands before she could say no. I took the cartoon out of the envelope. In the cartoon, there was a building marked PLANNED PARENTHOOD. Attached to it was another building marked CAFÉ and DELI. There were tables and chairs in front of the buildings, and at one table sat a man and a woman. The man was holding what seemed to be a sandwich and was saying to the woman, "I know it looks like a hamburger, Doris. But it doesn't taste like any hamburger *I've* ever eaten."

I stared at the cartoon for a long time, trying to figure out what to say about it. Finally, my ex-wife must have taken my silence for confusion, because she said, "Meaning instead of a hamburger, it was a fetus."

Then I looked up at her, and saw that her face was shining and wide-open and hopeful, and also not caring much whether I saw all those things on her face or not, and I fell in love with her a little again, still.

"It's really good," I said. "I think you should send it to the *New Yorker*."

She nodded. "I already have," she said.

I couldn't believe it. "When?" I said. "How?"

But this reminded me of the end of a big argument we'd had at the end our marriage. "Are you really going to leave me?" I'd asked her.

"I already have," she'd said.

I couldn't believe it. "When?" I'd said. "How?" But what I'd thought was, *Oh, I miss you so much*, and I thought it now, too. But I didn't say that. I just handed back her cartoon and walked into the community center. Since I'd taken that cartoon-drawing class, I'd taken a class in photography, and then a class in boatbuilding. Now I was taking a class in mapmaking and, in fact, was holding my own manila envelope.

In it was a map I'd drawn of Portland, Maine, in 1921. This was what we did in mapmaking class: we drew maps of places that had already been mapped. All the maps had already been drawn, except we pretended that they hadn't.

# Children Who Divorce

B efore they find Lisa in the river, before the doctor goes to prison, before any of what happens happens . . . it is just a normal pre-matinee August afternoon, and there we are, us five cast members in our costumes, sitting in the room next to the boiler, talking about our divorces; and there he is, the doctor, faraway in the eyes, not listening to us, thinking about something else.

"You're not listening to us," we tell him. "You're thinking about something else."

"I'm not," he says, but he is. Maybe he's thinking about the other casts he's doctored. Maybe he's thinking about the cast from three years ago, the cast of *The Sound of Music: After Edelweiss*, the kids who, after escaping the Nazis on film, grew up and became members of hate groups in real life, and who, backstage, after the curtain had dropped, kept asking the ushers and usherettes if there were any "mudpeople" in the audience. Maybe he's thinking of the cast from two years ago, the cast of *Where, Oh Where, Is Peter Pan?* about Michael and John and Wendy, who onstage had stopped believing in Neverland and offstage had started believing in the needle drugs. Or maybe he's thinking of last year's cast, of *No Longer Little Orphan Annie*, six feet tall in her red Afro flecked with gray, addicted to child pornography. Maybe he's thinking of her onstage, still singing about her hard-knock life, while after the show, backstage, she's on her laptop computer, looking at we don't want to know what. Maybe, if we'd been there, we'd be thinking about that, too. But we weren't there, and we're not that kind of cast with those kinds of problems: we were once the cast of *Willy Wonka & the Chocolate Factory*, and now we're the cast of *Trouble at the Chocolate Factory: Strike!* and in between, we all got married and then divorced, and now we want to talk about it—again, again—and we want the doctor to listen.

"I'm listening," he says. Just then, we hear the all-aboard whistle, we hear the thunder of feet on the gangplank, we hear the boiler fire and roar, we hear the paddle wheels begin to turn, we hear the waves from the paddle wheels turning start to *fwap* against the concrete landing, and we hear the heavy iron chains creaking and straining against the force of the paddle wheels, struggling to keep the boat moored to the concrete landing. We know soon someone will come downstairs, knock on the door, and say, "Five minutes 'til curtain," and before that happens we need to say what we need to say. About how we all fell in love with Gene Wilder when he was our Willy Wonka and we were his fat German, his spoiled heiress, his gum chewer, his gun-crazy American, his good-hearted Charlie Bucket. That we all married men and woman who looked like Mr. Wilder, and then divorced them because they just weren't him, they weren't what or who we were missing, no matter who they looked like. That even now, thirty years later, we still think about the jaunty angle of Mr. Wilder's top hat; his unruly, matted side-parted hair; his dashing cane; the cut of his tapered pants; his gentle way with the Oompa Loompas. That we wish, when people ask us why we got divorced, we could say, "Because she cheated on me," or "Because he got drunk and beat me with a piece of garden hose," and not because he or she didn't live up to the standard of a man with whom we spent six weeks thirty years ago. That we sometimes wish we'd never met Mr. Wilder, and that other times we wish we'd never met anyone else. We say all this in a rush, before the doctor can interrupt us, and by the time we're done, we're exhausted, wrung out; our lederhosen are drooping, our gum-chomping jaws weary, our supposedly sweatproof costumes completely sweated through. We look as though we've just been pulled out of the Ohio River, and we know what someone looks like when they've just been pulled out of the Ohio River, because we are there five hours later when Lisa is pulled out of the Ohio River, except when that happens, she's dead, whereas we're just divorced grown-up child actors who've sweated through our supposedly sweatproof costumes.

There's a knock on the door; it opens a crack, and Lisa's face fills part of the crack. She's wearing the famous purple top hat, her curly brown hair pouring out from underneath. Her face is sprayed-on tan and buttery. We can hear her tap, tap, tapping her cane against the outside of the door, which we know she does when she's about to go on and is nervous. But she doesn't *look* nervous: she smiles at us reassuringly, as though we're still child actors who need to be reassured. "Five minutes 'til curtain," Lisa says, then leans a little farther into the room and peeks around the door at the doctor. "Hello, you," she says, still smiling, then turns and closes the door behind her, leaving a waft of her aggressively masculine cologne—somewhere between musk and metal shop—as befits a woman who is playing a man who is trying to make the audience, and for that matter, her fellow cast members, believe she is a man, and not a woman playing a man. So far, we've heard no complaints from the audience and we have no complaints ourselves. Lisa isn't Mr. Wilder, but she's not bad. And for some people, we know she's more than just not bad. The doctor stares at the door with soft eyes, as though the door has just said the sweetest thing to him. He looks at the door the way we looked at Mr. Wilder, the way we want someone to look at us.

"She's something special, isn't she?" we ask him.

He doesn't take his eyes off the door. "I don't think I know what you mean," he says. But we think he does.

THIS ALL HAPPENS on the *Ohio River Lady Queen*, a four-story steam-powered paddleboat that in the golden age of four-story steam-powered paddleboats (we're quoting directly from the Ohio River Lady Queen Players' program) hauled its passengers and their steamer trunks from Cincinnati to Memphis to New Orleans and then back again. Now the *Ohio River Lady Queen* is docked in the Port of Cincinnati, where each summer it hosts a nightly dinner theater. Five years ago, we've been told, it was like any other summer dinner theater held on any other boat docked on any other river. Five years ago, the nowhere-near-capacity audience paid their thirty dollars to eat their prime rib or vegetarian lasagna or broiled cod while watching just-graduated theater majors from the local state college refine their Conrad Birdies and Blanche DuBoises. Five years ago, the only difference between this floating dinner theater and any other was that aboard the *Ohio River Lady Queen*, each show ended with a song from *Big River*, whether or not the show was a musical, which it usually was, and whether or not the show had anything to do with the Ohio River itself, or water at all, which it usually did not.

That was five years ago, before the theater and boat were bought by a former Cincinnati mayor, who, having been impeached after paying a lap dancer with a city check, became obsessed with his second act. And his second act, it turns out, was to establish a floating dinner theater that produced updated theatrical versions of famous movies and plays (all of which he wrote himself, with the help of his former team

of speechwriters) featuring the grown-up child actors who'd
starred in the originals. It worked, too. The theater has been
sold-out for four years running, five nights and two matinees
a week, every July and August. The only public hitch was the
first year, when the kids from *Swiss Family Robinson: Back in
Civilization* began to sing a song that wasn't in the script—the
show wasn't even a musical—a song sung in tongues about,
apparently, how the whores, boozers, and jewelers of Zurich
would burn in hell and how very sorry they'd be to miss out
on the Rapture. That's when the doctor was hired, to watch
out for the cast, to talk to us in between shows, to make sure
we get whatever is in our system out of our system before we
get onstage. That was four years ago; the doctor has been on
board ever since. Every afternoon, before every show, we meet
in group, as required by our contracts. Every night, the doctor
sits in the front row, watching the show, as required by his con-
tract. There hasn't been a problem in all that time, until now.

AFTER THE SHOW but before Lisa drowns in the river,
we do what we've done after every show for the month we've
been on the *Ohio River Lady Queen*: we retreat to the room next
to the boiler, get on our cell phones and call home—our children, our ex-wives and ex-husbands, our on-and-off girlfriends
and boyfriends if we have them, our parents if they're still
alive, whomever it is we have who we can call *home* when we
call home—and tell them about the show: about power-mad
and despotic Charlie and about the solidarity of the formerly

downtrodden and now unionized Oompa Loompas—their strike songs, their placards, their hatred of the scabs who are supposed to be shorter, more desperate Africans imported by Charlie from an even more obscure, more desperate part of Africa. We tell them about the other four of us, no longer gluttonous, greedy, violent, voracious, all of us reformed except for our costumes, which are adult-sized versions of what we wore thirty years ago, summoned by Wonka—who has come out of retirement, tanned from self-imposed exile in The Islands (the script doesn't say which ones)—to the factory to show Charlie the error of his ways and to rediscover the true spirit of candy, which, of course, in the grand finale he finds with the help of the song "The True Spirit of Candy." We tell them about how the kids playing the scabs—four- and five-year-olds all, except for an especially runtish six-year-old or two—are too young, too inexperienced to be in a show of this caliber, how they flub their lines and bang into each other during the choreographed numbers, how they actually fall and get trampled in the strike scene in which they're supposed to pretend to fall and get trampled. We tell them about our little triumphs: how we ad-libbed and spit into the vat of milk chocolate instead of "looking evil" as the script told us to do, how we performed seamlessly during the dance scenes, how the audience just marveled at how unified we were, not individual actors but a group, not five "I's" but one "we." We do not tell them how the audience gasped when they saw us, saw the thirty years that had passed since the last time we'd been seen and how completely different we looked except for our costumes. Instead, we tell them Lisa did fine, was perfectly adequate, even though she of course was no Mr. Wilder, that of course there is no Mr. Wilder except for Mr. Wilder himself. And then they tell us, before we can ask, because they know we will, that no, Mr. Wilder hasn't called to say he's heard about the show (the adult stars are never asked to be part of the Ohio Lady Queen Players, because they are too famous, or too old, or too dead) and to offer us his congratulations. "That's OK," we say. "He's probably busy." "Probably," they say. And then: "Have you gotten paid yet?" We say that we get paid at the end of the week and we'll send them money soon, because—as we don't need to tell them, nor they us—we haven't worked in a while, and the alimony and child support payments and the mortgages on our condos in the desert (we all live in condos in the desert) are overdue and overdue again. "Promise you'll send us money," they tell us. "We promise," we promise. Then, whoever we call when we call home hangs up, and we're left with each other.

All of us except for Lisa. She's younger than us by twenty years (that's another part of the show—how Wonka gets younger and the children get older—that the script doesn't attempt to explain). After the show, she doesn't call anyone. Is she too young to have someone at home? When she was even younger, did she have her own Mr. Wilder to think about for the rest of her days? Is it possible that she didn't? Is it possible that not everyone has their own Mr. Wilder, that it's only us? This is something we talk about all the time in group: Are we normal? Are there others like us? Is everyone like us? Or are we all alone? Lisa isn't part of group because, of course, she wasn't a child actor, just a niece of the big boss with some experience in community theater, who isn't as brilliant as Mr. Wilder but isn't nearly as terrible as maybe we want her to be.

In any case, Lisa waits out in the hall until we've been hung up on by whomever we have at home. Then, she comes into the boiler room, her bottled tan streaked a little, her pretty curls dented and flattened by the purple top hat.

"Great show, guys," she says, because she calls us "guys." She has an open bottle of champagne in each hand. Past casts have been forbidden by her uncle to drink at all, but not us: we're not the kind of cast with a drinking problem, and so we can drink a glass or two of champagne after a show without the big boss or the doctor having to worry about what will happen to us, or the show, or the ship. But not between the matinee and the evening show; never between the matinee and the evening show. Lisa raises both bottles above her head and shakes them party-hearty style, which is the universal dinner theater actor symbol for "trouble." "You guys were *really* great," she says.

"Thank you," we say. "You were pretty good, too."

"Thank you," she says, her face pinched, obviously a little wounded by the "pretty good," which is what we intended.

"Where's the doctor?" we ask her.

"I don't know," she says, shrugging her shoulders. "Who knows where he is?"

"Who knows?" we repeat. Maybe tonight she really *doesn't* know where he is. But on every other night for the past month, Lisa would have known where the doctor was, and so would we: he would have been somewhere on the boat, waiting for her. Picture it. Every night, we're in our cabins, trying to sleep, listening to the river gently rocking and splashing the boat, listening to the chugging of the coal barges, to the tooting of the tugboats, listening to the moaning and creaking of the old *Lady Queen* herself. But still, even over all that racket, we can hear the doctor and Lisa. We can hear them in the boiler room; we can hear them behind the smokestacks on the upper deck; we can hear them backstage; we can hear them the way we can hear Mr. Wilder and ourselves from thirty years ago. They think we can't hear them, but we can. They think we haven't seen them, but we have. They think we don't know, but we do.

"You think we don't know," we tell Lisa. "But we do."

WE MET THE doctor's wife only once, our first day on board the *Ohio River Lady Queen*, at the party when the cast was to meet the crew for the first time, etc. She was pretty enough, pale but not sickly, with long straight blonde hair, and wearing that sort of shapeless sundress that pregnant women wear when they don't want people to know they're pregnant, or that nonpregnant thin women wear when they don't want people to know they have bodies that someone might want to look at. She was clearly the latter. When we first saw her,

across the boat's upper deck, she was standing next to her husband, the doctor (we hadn't met him yet, but we knew he was
our doctor because we'd had many other doctors and they all
looked like him, he like them), who looked bookish in his blue
corduroy jacket, his salt-and-pepper beard, his chewed-on pens
sticking out of his shirt pocket. She looked bookish, too, the
sort of woman who, when she got older, would wear bifocals
around her neck on a chain. They were standing next to each
other, close but not actually touching. The doctor kept leaning
toward her, just barely, and the doctor's wife kept leaning away
from him, just barely. Once, twice, three times, the doctor
walked away to talk to someone else—someone from the crew
or administration he'd known for four years now but probably
someone his wife didn't know at all—and each time, right
before he left, her look changed, almost imperceptibly except
we perceived it, and it said, *Why don't you go?* And when he
came back, her look said, *Why have you come back?* These are
exactly the kind of things we tend to notice. For us, the world
is divided between those who long and those who are longed
for, those who are defined by their longing, and those who
are totally oblivious to it. When the movie wrapped, we spent
weeks crying in our bedrooms; we once in a while stopped crying long enough to write long, rambling letters to Mr. Wilder,
telling him how much we missed him and how great the sequel
would be once he agreed to be in it. *You will agree to be in the
sequel, won't you?* we asked in the letters, and then we started
crying again, letting our tears stain the letters before we put

them in the mail. We have no idea if he got them or not. Mr. Wilder apparently went salmon fishing in Alaska with some buddies after we finished shooting. We never even got a post-card. There was never any sequel, until now. We've never seen Mr. Wilder again, except on television, in the movies, on the cover of his memoir, just like the rest of you.

When the doctor left his wife for the fourth time—to go to the bathroom, to get a drink, to talk to an old friend or make a new one—we went over and tried to talk to her ourselves.

"Your husband is our doctor," we said to her.

"I'm his wife," she said back.

We shook hands with the doctor's wife, said how nice it was to meet her. She said it was nice to meet us, too. After that, no one seemed to know *what* to say. The doctor's wife kept looking over and around us to see where the doctor was; when she wasn't looking for her husband, she looked at her watch. These two things seemed to be the only things she knew how to do. Finally, after who knows how long we spent standing there, watching her do these two things, we said, "You don't want to be here, do you?"

"What do you mean?"

"With your husband," we said. "We saw the way you kept leaning away from him. The way you looked at him."

"I have no idea what you're talking about," she said.

We didn't say anything back to that. We knew all about de-nying the obvious truth. For years, we'd denied that we missed Mr. Wilder. We denied that he was anything to us at all. That's why we got married, as soon as we were able to, at sixteen: to prove that he no longer mattered to us, that we'd moved on. When our friends and families pointed out that our new wives and husbands looked like Mr. Wilder, we denied it. When our new wives and husbands said, "You know, people say I look a lot like Gene Wilder," we said that it wasn't true. So, when the doctor's wife said that she had no idea what we were talking about, we knew all about it; we knew that there's no talking to a person like that, because we're that person and there's no talking to us, either.

"Just tell my husband I went home, will you?" she said. A waiter came by with a tray of cheese cubes, and she grabbed a handful and started popping them in her mouth like peanuts.

"We will," we said.

"Why do you talk like that?" she asked.

"Like what?" we said.

"We," she said. "You refer to yourselves as 'we.' Why?" And then, before we could tell her why, she turned, walked down the stairs, and was gone. We went to the railing—we were on the ship's upper deck—and watched her walk down the gangplank, into the parking lot, into her car; we watched her car climb up, up, up, away from the river and into the blinking hills of Cincinnati until it was gone. And we never saw her again until we saw her on the news, running past the cameras, refusing to say anything about her husband except that pretty soon he wouldn't be.

Then we turned and faced the rest of the party. The doctor

was on the other side of the boat, talking to a middle-aged
man and a young woman. The man was wearing a blue blazer
and a black polo shirt, and glasses that were meant to make
him look twenty years younger but instead made him look like
a middle-aged man who was wearing glasses meant to, etc.; the
woman was wearing a dress that was barely one, just strips of
white fabric somewhat covering the important places. This, as
it turns out, was the big boss and his new wife, who once upon
a time had been the lap dancer he'd paid with a city check.
They were both very tan, and their teeth were very white.
We introduced ourselves to the boss (we'd talked to him only
once, on the phone, when he'd offered us the job and we'd accepted), and to his wife, and then to the doctor we said, "We're
your patients."

"Good to meet you," he said, shaking hands with each of us.

"Your wife told us to tell you that she went home," we said.

"What?" he asked, and we repeated what she told us to tell
him. The doctor closed his eyes, lowered his head, and rubbed
the bridge of his nose for a little while. Finally, he opened his
eyes again, said, "Will you please excuse me?" and then, as his
wife had a done a few minutes earlier, he disappeared down
the stairs. We all stood there for a while, looking at the place
where the doctor had just been, until the big boss's wife said,
"Those poor kids. They've stopped thinking about their ideal
moment."

"Their ideal moment?" we said.

"Their ideal moment," she said. "Something you think about

all the time, an ideal moment you work toward achieving, even if you never actually achieve it. Every couple has to have one if they're going to stay together."

"They do," we said, seriously considering this, just as we have seriously considered other things over the years—hypnosis, insulin shock treatments, hyperbaric chambers, Outward Bound—anything to help us forget, or to help us remember but in the right way, or to help us do whatever it is other people do to make them different from us.

"They do," she said. "Do you want to hear mine?" And then she started to tell us before we could say whether we wanted to or not. "My guy makes me dinner, and for dessert, we do it all over the house: in the basement, in the shower, on the table, in the living room, in front of the mirror. After we christen every room, he carries me upstairs, to our bedroom, where we scream each other's name or say things like, 'You turn me on,' or 'You make me so hot.' I try to time it so we come together. When that's about to happen, we get into the missionary position. And then he pulls out and comes all over my stomach while we look into each other's eyes."

"Wow," we said.

"Wow," said the waiter, waiting for us to notice him and his tray of shrimp cocktail.

"Baby, I've never told you this," the big boss said, hooking his left arm around her waist, "but that's my ideal moment, too." He then started groping her, right there in front of us, but his wife fought him off.

"Not now, you big ape. I want to hear about *their* ideal moments." She hooked her thumb at us, and in doing so she got it caught in one of her thin straps of clothing, and then the big boss pretended to help her unhook it, and in doing so, undid the whole piece of fabric, and then they started laughing as they pretended to try to attach hook A to hook B. We had to turn our heads, not because we found the whole thing embarrassing, but because they were happy, and if you're unhappy, it's hard to look at other people being happy without wishing they weren't, and if you start wishing someone is unhappy, it's very hard to stop at just wishing.

"What were we talking about?" the big boss's wife finally said. We looked at her again and saw that she was back to being at least barely clothed, although the big boss had yet to totally untangle his hands from her straps and swaths yet.

"Their ideal moment," the big boss said.

"Oh, you wouldn't be interested," we said.

"I would," she said. "Try me."

So we tried her: for one of us, our ideal moment was sitting in a firelit room with Mr. Wilder, reading over our scripts, talking about our characters' motivations; for one of us, it was being in bed with her now ex-husband, making love to him, and then not thinking about Mr. Wilder immediately afterward; for another, it was the day he finally made his children understand why he'd left their mother and them and ruined their lives—because of Mr. Wilder—so that they could help him understand the same thing. We said all this not together but as individuals, talking over each other, shouting when talking wasn't loud enough, making less and less sense the more we talked. Because this was the answer to the doctor's wife's question—*Why do you talk that way?* Individually we sounded like Babel, but together we sounded like a chorus. Individually, we were ridiculous, pathetic; but together, we were a group of ridiculous, pathetic people who—as five and not just one—had a certain amount of authority, like a club, or a focus group, or a jury. Individually, someone might feel sorry for us; but together, someone might feel scared. That was our hope, pretty much our last one. In any case, when we finally finished talking about our ideal moments, the big boss took off his glasses, as if we were an even worse cast than the ones who'd come before us and he couldn't bear to look at us. He even untangled his hands from his wife's thin strips of clothing, as if our ideal moments had made him forget all about his, and hers. His wife was clearly feeling the same way: she covered her mouth with her hand, and through the hand she said, "You were just babies. What did that sick man do to you?"

"No, no. It wasn't that way at all," we said, because other people had also assumed it was that way, and because it wasn't.

"Then what way was it?"

"It's hard to say," we said, because it was.

"What's hard to say?" the doctor said, coming up from behind us.

We turned to face him, and we must have had that look on our face that said, *Help us, You're the only one who can help us.*

*Please help us!* because he took a step back, buttoned his jacket, and took one of his pens out of his pocket as though preparing to take notes—in other words, he'd made himself look less like a man who had his own troubles, which might make him better understand ours, and more like every other doctor who'd tried to help us and failed—and we all of a sudden felt tired, so very tired. So we excused ourselves, said we had an early rehearsal the next day and that we were worn-out from our flights, from the time change, and went below deck to our rooms and tried to get some sleep, which we could not do. We could not sleep. Because hope is the thing that keeps you from sleeping, and all we could think of was the doctor and his wife and how maybe, if we saw the doctor again with his professional guard down, then we'd see him as someone more like us than he wanted to admit, someone who really might help us. So we crept up to the top deck and saw the doctor with his professional guard down. He was standing at the far end of the deck, leaning on the railing, holding a bottle of beer by the neck, talking to Lisa. There was no one else on the deck, and the moon, which was full or close to it, shone on them, on the deck, on the river, on everything. He was clearly a happier, less worried doctor than he'd been earlier: we could tell that already he was in love with Lisa. He had a huge, toothy smile that said: *I can't believe I'm already in love with her.* Lisa had the same smile on her face. We'd been introduced to her earlier, said a few strained but pleasant words to her, but all we could see of Lisa was that she wasn't Mr. Wilder. But we could see, now, the way the doctor was seeing her, and we also saw that she was the kind of person who almost made you wish your heart hadn't already been broken so that she could break it for you, almost made you forget the person who'd broken it in the first place. And we could see that he was just another doctor in a long line of doctors, another doctor to whom you would tell your story and hope that he could help you understand something about what you wanted and why you wanted it and how you might then get what you wanted. But in the end he couldn't. And what do you do when you don't get what you want? You do the only thing you can. You make sure no one else gets what they want, either.

"OH, WE THINK you know what we mean," we say to the doctor. This is after Lisa has told us it's five minutes 'til curtain but before the matinee itself, before she gets drunk on champagne afterward, before she ends up dead in the river.

"What *do* you mean?" the doctor says, trying so hard to act like he doesn't know what we're talking about, to act like whatever we're about to tell him is someone else's problem and he's only there to solve it, to act like the doctor. But we don't want him to be the doctor anymore; we want him to be scared, nervous, ashamed, defiant, weak, helpless. We want him to be everything no one wants to be. We want him to be like us. So we tell him everything—everything we know about him and Lisa, everything we've seen, everything we've heard—and while he listens, he stares at the ceiling, chews on his pen, nods a little bit. When we're through telling him what we know, the doctor looks at us and says, "OK, so you know. Good for you. So what?"

"It's wrong," we say. "That's so what."

"Lisa isn't my patient," he says. "She's not one of you. And I love her."

"It's still wrong," we tell him, and he doesn't deny it.

"Love makes you do things you shouldn't," he says, and it's clear that he's prepared, rehearsed for a moment like this. Because part of being in love is practicing the way you'll talk about it to people who will tell you it's wrong, or that it's not love at all.

"You're married," we tell him.

"So were you," he says. Because after all, he's our doctor, and he knows a few things about us, too, and one of the things he knows is that we cheated on our wives and husbands, too, once we figured out they weren't who we were looking for. All of us were cheaters before we were legally able to vote, divorced before we were legally able to drink. The doctor knows all of this. "All of you were married, and all of you did the same thing," he says.

"We didn't love them," we tell him, which he also knows.

"Neither do I," he says.

"So you're just like us," we say.

"I'm not," he says, and here he smiles. It's a deep, satisfied, mean smile. We know what's coming next: every doctor we've ever known longs for the moment when his patients are no longer his patients, and he can either declare the patients cured or he can declare his patients hopeless and then tell them exactly what he thinks of them. "You got divorced because of some guy—an *actor*—who barely knew you thirty years ago. This guy doesn't even know you exist anymore; he barely knew you existed in the first place. Why do you even want him to know? Why do you care? Even you have no idea. How many doctors later and you still have no idea. The best you can do is walk around in your sad little group, freaking everybody out, talking about your divorces. And why do you care about *that*? People get married and divorced all the time. Every day."

"Not like us," we say. "Not for reasons like ours."

"That's what I'm saying," the doctor says. " My reasons aren't like your reasons. I have Lisa. I'm not like you at all."

"Poor Lisa," we say, because we'd rehearsed for this moment, too: we talked about it beforehand, prepared for it; because we're actors and we know exactly what to do, what to say, whom to say it to, and when to say it.

"Poor Lisa why?"

"Poor Lisa told us about you."

"She didn't," the doctor says.

"She did," we say, even though she didn't. "She told us how she feels, being with you." We wait for the doctor to ask us how she feels, but he doesn't: he just stares at us, defiantly, as if daring us to tell us something that isn't true. So we do. "She told us that she feels like a whore."

"She didn't say that," the doctor shouts, his voice catching a little bit, and then, because maybe shouting isn't enough, he stands up. Strangely, he has less power over us standing up than he has when he's sitting down with his legs crossed, which is how he normally sits in group.

"We're sorry, but she did," we say. "She says she feels like a whore, sleeping with a married man. Those were her very words."

"But I won't be a married man," he says. We can hear the desperation now: because you're never more desperate when you argue with the truth, or with what you're told is the truth. "I'm getting a divorce. I've told her that. She *knows* that."

"We know," we say. "That makes her feel even more like a whore, wrecking your marriage for her. It makes her want to kill herself."

"She said that?" the doctor says. He's totally given himself over to our truth by now. Because we're good. This is exactly what Mr. Wilder said about us, once, to the director—"Those kids are good"—which is another reason we can't forget about him: he was the first person to tell us we were good. If you want someone to forget you, never be the first person to tell them that they are good, at anything. Because if you tell them that once, they'll keep wanting you to tell them, and if you don't, they'll never stop wondering why.

"She really did," we say. "We told her to never say it again. And then she said it again. We think she means it. We think she might really kill herself if you don't leave your wife."

"But she loves me," the doctor says.

"Yes, she does. Very much," we tell him. "That just makes it worse for her, you know."

The doctor drops his head, because he does know. He knows exactly what we're talking about, knows the rest of the story without having to hear the rest of the story, knows exactly what the right thing is, what he has to do, what he will do. Because there are only a few stories (the Ohio River Lady Queen Players are a floating dinner-serving testament to that truth) and everyone knows them, everyone knows exactly how they go, not because they're predictable or boring, but because they're true, or because they so easily could be.

Just then, we hear the big boss over the loudspeaker, telling everyone that the show will start in a minute and to please take their seats, and so we get up out of ours and head for the door. The doctor has stopped paying attention to us. He just sits there, looking blankly at the wall as though there are words on it, instructions that he can't believe are meant for him to follow.

"'YOU THINK WE don't know. But we do,'" Lisa says, mimicking us. She takes a big slug from one of the bottles of champagne, closes her eyes against the taste, then opens them again. "'We. We. We.' You don't know one thing about me," she says.

"We know lots of things," and then we tell her everything we told the doctor just a few hours earlier.

"Do you know that I love him?" she says. "That he loves me, too, no matter what he says?"

"We do know that," we say. And then: "Why? What does he say?" Even though we know what he's said. We know that after the matinee, before the champagne, the doctor told Lisa that it was over between them, that he couldn't see her anymore, that it was better this way. We know this as though it were a script we'd written ourselves, know it as though we were there when it happened, know it as though Lisa tells us so herself, which she does not do. All she says is, "I love him. I just love him. That's all I know."

"We know, we know," we say. "We know all about it."

She nods, takes another slug from the bottle, then closes her eyes again and keeps them closed for a long time. Maybe she's thinking what we're thinking: about the rest of her life, about how she won't be able to forget him, no matter what she does to forget him. We know the feeling. We know exactly how it'll go; she's just like us, and now that she's just like us, we feel a little less like us ourselves. Lisa's eyes are still closed, and she starts leaning forward, as though she's going to fall right on her face. Her cane leans in the corner, far out of her reach. It won't be there to catch her if she falls, and neither will we. We want her to fall. *Fall,* we tell her. *Rise,* we tell ourselves.

Except she doesn't fall, and we don't rise. Just at the moment when it seems as though Lisa is going to really fall, really hurt herself, really embarrass herself, she tucks her head between her legs, executes a perfect roll, and pops up on her feet, a triumphant look lighting up her face. It's just like Mr. Wilder's famous tumble in the movie, except it's better: because this isn't a movie, because it wasn't rehearsed, because Mr. Wilder didn't have us there wanting him to fall and hurt himself, and because Lisa didn't even spill a drop of champagne while doing it.

"Life goes on," she says. "Who wants a drink?"

There are two famous pictures of us, both in the same magazine. One, a picture of when we all got married, and one, a few years later, after we'd announced we were getting divorced. Over the first was the headline HOLLYWOOD CHILDREN WHO MARRY! Over the second was the headline HOLLYWOOD CHILDREN WHO DIVORCE! But we looked the same in both pictures: too young; full of longing; jealous of the people who were taking our pictures and who weren't us; jealous of anyone, everything. So jealous. One day in group, the doctor said, "You're so jealous."

"Of what?" we asked.

"Of everything," he said. He was right, but he never did tell us what to do about it. What do you do if you're so jealous? What do you do when a person has done in one minute—*Life goes on!*—what you haven't been able to do in thirty years? Do you try to stop feeling so jealous, or do you get rid of the things you might be jealous of?

"We do," we tell Lisa. "We'd love a drink!" She gives us one, then another, then another, her drinking two for each of our one. When we're all good and drunk, we tell her how much we admired her roll, how it was better even than Mr. Wilder's, but how much better yet it would be if she could do it somewhere other than this cramped little room, somewhere with more space, like the upper deck, where no one was likely to be between shows, where she could have all the space she needed, and where we'd be her audience, the last one she'd ever know, the next-to-last one she'd ever have.

THE POLICE USE a net to pull Lisa out of the river and onto the concrete landing. The people who matter most (the five of us, the big boss, the doctor) stand close to them, to her. The rest of you (the crew, the ushers and usherettes, the understudies, the people who came to the boat thinking they'd see one show and ended up seeing another one, the city itself, its houses and the people in them) are obscure in the dark behind us, watching us. Our audience. We wonder if you see Lisa as we see her: her hair is wet; her skin is chalky; her lips are as purple as Mr. Wilder's famous purple hat. We wonder if you see Lisa as the big boss sees her: not so much his poor dead niece, but as the end of his second act and the beginning of whatever his third act might be. We wonder if you see her as the doctor sees her: as the woman he'll never stop loving, never stop thinking about, never stop feeling guilty about. Never, ever, ever. We wonder if you see her as the police see her: as a body to take out of the net, to put in the wagon, to take to the morgue. We wonder if you see us as the police see us, as we make the police see us: as Lisa's castmates, her confidants, five people to whom she would have told everything, five people the police can trust to tell them the things Lisa told no one else. We wonder if you see the doctor as the police see him:

as Lisa's lover, her married lover, about whom—as a married lover—everything is already known. We wonder if you feel the chills we feel when we tell the police what the doctor told us earlier, after one of the ushers spotted Lisa's body in the river: "Oh my god, I killed her." We wonder if you know what we know: that love makes you do things you shouldn't, that grief and guilt make you confess to things you haven't done. We wonder—after you've seen the police handcuff the doctor and haul him away, after the show is over and you assume there is nothing left to see—if you notice the five of us still standing there, waiting for something, someone. We wonder if you know that we're waiting for one of you to come out of the audience, out of the years and years of waiting, and to call us by our names and tell us that we've been on your mind, in your heart, and that we're as good as we ever were, each and every one of us.

# The Pity Palace

................................................................

**A**ntonio Vieri's wife had left him for the famous American author who wrote those best-selling novels about Italian gangsters in New York, and Antonio Vieri was feeling sorry for himself, so very sorry for himself that his friends warned him that if he did not stop feeling sorry for himself, he, Antonio Vieri, would become famous for it throughout Florence (they lived in Florence), the way the Uffizi was famous for its Michelangelo, Il Duomo for its *duomo*.

"This is not possible," Antonio Vieri said. "I do not ever leave my apartment." This was true. Antonio Vieri hadn't left his apartment since his wife had left him for the famous American author. The only thing he did was eat the food his friends brought him and read the famous American author's best-selling novels about Italian gangsters in New York. They had once been Antonio Vieri's wife's novels, and she had loved them, and he had loved that she'd loved them, until finally she loved the novels too much, for too long, and he got jealous and told her that if she loved the novels so much, then maybe she should leave him for the famous American author who wrote them. And so she did that. Now that his wife was gone, Antonio Vieri read the best-selling novels himself. Maybe there was something in the best-selling novels that might help him get her back. That was his hope, his plan. It would work, too; of this, Antonio Vieri was certain: it would work, because it had to. Until it did, Antonio Vieri was going to stay in his apartment and read the best-selling novels and eat the food his friends brought him and feel sorry for himself, and nothing or no one could convince him to do otherwise. He told his friends, "I cannot become famous for anything if I don't leave my apartment."

"You are wrong," his friends told him. "We are warning you."

"But I miss her so much," Antonio Vieri said.

"We know, we know," they said.

"I miss everything about her," Antonio Vieri said. "I even miss the way she ate her *insalata mista*."

"You must stop this," his friends said.

"She ate her *insalata mista* so delicately, one leaf at a time," Antonio Vieri said. "She ate her *insalata mista* like an *angel*."

"We've warned you," his friends told Antonio Vieri. "Don't say we didn't warn you."

"Go—what is the expression?—fornicate with your own bodies," he told them. Antonio Vieri had learned this expression from the famous American author's best-selling novels about Italian gangsters in New York. Antonio Vieri could speak and read English adequately, but he could only find the novels in their Italian translations. Sometimes, Antonio Vieri wondered about the accuracy of the translations, especially of the American vernacular.

"What?" his friends asked. "What did you tell us to do with our bodies?"

"Please just go away," he said.

"For how long?" they asked.

"Forever," he said.

"Gladly," they said. "But don't forget that we warned you," and then they disappeared into the place in hell reserved for friends who think they know best.

ONCE HIS FRIENDS had gone away, Antonio Vieri was alone. All alone! Antonio Vieri remembered the last time he was all alone. This was before he'd found his wife, his friends. He had been sitting in this very same apartment, surrounded by these same cracked plaster walls, without even the famous American author's best-selling novels about Italian gangsters in New York to keep him company, and he'd said to himself, out loud, in the manner of the truly lonely, "Antonio Vieri, if you do not find a wife, if you do not find friends, then you are going to end up in this apartment all alone for the rest of your life. You are going to end up as the saddest man in Florence. I am warning you." That was a bad feeling, and it had caused

Antonio Vieri to find himself a wife and friends. But now Antonio Vieri's wife had left him and he'd told his friends to go away, and this feeling was much worse: the only thing worse than being all alone was to have some other way of being to which to compare your loneliness, and then to lose it. All alone again, after not being all alone for a little while! Antonio Vieri ran to the window, with the intention of throwing it open and shouting to his friends, "Come back. I am all alone again. Please come back!" But once Antonio Vieri got to the window, he saw something in the piazza below that made him forget about his friends. It was the famous American author who'd written those best-selling novels about Italian gangsters in New York, sitting at an outdoor café, drinking red wine. Out of all the outdoor cafés in all the piazzas in all of Florence, the famous American author had to drink red wine in this one, and he'd been out there every day since Antonio Vieri's wife had left him. As for Antonio Vieri's wife, he had not seen her since she'd left him. But then again, the Italian gangsters in New York liked to keep their women out of sight; Antonio Vieri assumed this was true of the famous American author who wrote best-selling novels about them, as well. That it *was* the famous American author, Antonio Vieri had no doubt: even though Antonio Vieri was four stories up, and the famous American author was sitting at the far edge of the piazza, it was definitely him, definitely the same man whose photo was on the back cover of the novels. He was the sort of fat man whose neck wouldn't permit the top two shirt buttons to be buttoned; he was bald, except for a wild swoop of thin hair meant to cover up the baldness; his glasses were so big, the lenses so thick, he could have worn them while welding. Yes, it was definitely the famous American author in the piazza drinking red wine, taunting Antonio Vieri just by sitting there. Antonio Vieri almost shook his fist in anger at the famous American author. But, no, that would be feeble, most feeble, especially since Antonio Vieri was four stories up and the famous American author was sitting at the far edge of the piazza and wouldn't be likely to see the fist-shaking. Besides, why shake your fist at the man who'd stolen your wife, when instead you could read the man's best-selling novels and find a way to get her back? So Antonio Vieri turned away from the window and did that.

THE NEXT DAY, Antonio Vieri was reading one of the famous American author's best-selling novels—*The Patriarch of the Gangsters* was the title, in translation—and trying to decide which of the character types his wife might want him to become if she were to return to him (hotheaded or levelheaded? red-blooded or cold-blooded? black-hearted or yellow-bellied?) when he heard a knock on the door. Antonio Vieri wondered who it could be. If it was his wife, he would welcome her back, no questions asked, and ask her to forgive his appearance, which was gruesomely unkempt and pathetic in the way of all jilted, self-pitying men. If it was his friends, and they had groceries for him, then Antonio Vieri would let them in, also no questions asked, and eat their food, and then, if they started warning him again about how, if he didn't watch out, he would become famous for self-pity, Antonio Vieri would ask them to go away again, forever, until the next time he was hungry. If it was the famous American author, Antonio Vieri would—what was the expression?—strike him with an athletic stick until he was murdered.

But it wasn't his wife, or his friends, or the famous American author. Instead, standing in the hallway, was a young man, an American who looked like—what was the expression?—a fragment of excrement. His hair was unwashed and brown, or brown because it was unwashed, but in any case it was dirty, so very dirty that it wouldn't lie quietly on his head but instead rose to a filthy, bristling ridge of hair, as on the back of a certain type of fighting dog or on the head of a certain type of fighting cock. When the American shucked his overlarge backpack (there was a Canadian flag patch stitched on the backpack, which was how Antonio Vieri knew he was an American), there were thick lines of sweat on his T-shirt where the straps had just been. The sweat-striped T-shirt was gray but had likely once been white and, in any case, was adorned with a banana and a thick-bodied worm, facing each other, apparently about to do battle. Both the banana and the worm had two eyes and a mouth and two arms and, at the end of the arms, overlarge black boxing gloves. The banana was haughty, the worm irate—this was conveyed through their eyes, their mouths. Underneath the banana and the worm were the letters UCSC. Antonio Vieri understood that the *U* and the *S* stood for

"United States," but he couldn't understand what the *C* and the other *C* signified, and why one was placed between the *U* and the *S*. Perhaps the banana was responsible for the disorder of the letters, and perhaps that explained why the worm was so furious with the banana. This American smelled, too, of something rotten, only partly obscured by something chemical and sweet. The smell was considerable and stood between them, like the door would have if Antonio Vieri hadn't already opened it.

"Are you Antonio Vieri?" the American asked.

"It is I," Antonio Vieri said. It seemed fruitless to deny it, especially since on the door, next to the number of his apartment (8) was his name: ANTONIO VIERI.

"Excellent," the American said. "How much?"

"How much?"

"Yes," the American said. "What will it cost for you to let me inside?" He said this slowly, as though Antonio Vieri didn't understand English, or as though there were something wrong with Antonio Vieri's head, which was, in fact, the case. Antonio Vieri was so hungry he couldn't think correctly: all he could think about was food, food, and how he didn't care if his friends brought it to him, or if it was just some filthy American who wanted, for some reason, to enter his apartment.

"Do you have any food?"

This American nodded, shucked his backpack, unzipped its front pocket, and removed something in a shiny metallic wrapper. Antonio Vieri took the object from this American, unwrapped it, saw that it was something candy-bar-like, but granular and thus probably better for you. He shoved the thing into his mouth, waved the American into his apartment, and shut the door behind them. The American immediately began walking around the apartment. He looked at the two framed and mounted caricatures of Antonio Vieri's wife—in one of them, she was eating *insalata mista* delicately, one leaf at a time, like an angel; in the other she was reading the famous American author's best-selling novels about Italian gangsters in New York—both of which Antonio Vieri had drawn himself, crudely but with all his heart. The American gently ran his hands over the piles of unwashed clothes on the floor, on the back of Antonio Vieri's chair, on his couch, on his kitchen table; he walked into the bedroom and sat on the bed, the bed that Antonio Vieri hadn't slept in since his wife had left him; he opened the faucet and ran the water over the unwashed dishes and cups. The American picked up the paperback copies of the famous American author's best-selling novels about Italian gangsters in New York, all nine of them, all of them read and reread so many times that they looked like something that had been punished. At one point, the American dropped his own healthy candy bar, bent down to pick it up, and then stayed there, on his haunches, looking for a long time at the dusty wooden floors, as though Antonio Vieri were a snail and the American could see the trails of self-pity Antonio Vieri had made as he'd dragged himself around the apartment.

"Wow," the American said.

"My wife has left me for the famous American author," Antonio Vieri said by way of apology and explanation.

"Yeah, yeah. I know that," the American said.

"You do?" he asked. "How?"

The American answered by pulling a piece of paper out of his backpack and handing it to Antonio Vieri; it was a mimeographed flyer that read:

NOW OPEN TO THE GENERAL PUBLIC:
The Pity Palace, home of Antonio Vieri, the saddest man in Florence. His wife left him for the famous American author who wrote those best-selling novels about Italian gangsters in New York. Please pity him.

Antonio Vieri knew who was responsible: his friends. *Those—what was the expression?—diseased conjugal acts,* thought Antonio Vieri. He wished he could bring his friends back so that he could tell them to go away again, but this time more forcefully.

"Where did you get this?" Antonio Vieri asked.

"A bunch of old coots were handing them out, outside the Piazza della Repubblica."

"Old what?" Antonio Vieri asked. "Coots" he didn't know. But *old*? He had never thought of his friends as old, which is to say that he'd never thought of himself as old, either. Antonio Vieri had always imagined he and his friends were more or less the same age. "Am I an—what is the expression?—old coot, too?"

"You sure are," the American said.

"Is that another reason my wife left me?" Antonio Vieri wondered. "Because I am an *old coot*?"

"It might be," the American said. "It's amazing. I feel better about myself just being in here."

"You do?"

"I do," the American said happily and wide-eyed, as though in a dream, the good kind. "My girlfriend dumped me two weeks ago. Not for anyone in particular, either. She said she'd rather be alone than with me. We were supposed to take this trip together, so I decided to go by myself. Yesterday, that seemed like a big mistake. Yesterday, I couldn't look at a naked statue—not even the guys—without thinking of her. But after being here, seeing you, I can't even remember what she looks like."

"I miss my wife so much," Antonio Vieri said automatically. "I miss the way she ate her *insalata mista*."

"Her what?"

"She ate her *insalata mista* so delicately, one leaf at a time," Antonio Vieri said. "She ate her *insalata mista* like an *angel*." He pointed in the direction of the caricatures; the American turned and looked at them once again, for a long time, his face shifting in phases—puzzlement, wonder, pity—before turning back to Antonio Vieri.

"Dude, did you draw those yourself?"

Antonio Vieri nodded. "Crudely," he said, "but with all my heart."

The American looked at Antonio Vieri the way, a moment earlier, he'd looked at the caricatures. Antonio Vieri could see the pity in his face, sloshing around in his eyes. The pity seemed to make the American taller, more erect, less sickly, as though the American were an undernourished plant and pity, just the right kind of plant food. He even smelled better, as though pity were the most effective type of deodorant.

"And she really left you for Mario Puzo?" the American asked.

"You are not allowed to refer to him by that name in this apartment!" Antonio Vieri shrieked. "You may call him 'the famous American author' or you may call him nothing at all." The way Antonio Vieri figured, the famous American author had something Antonio Vieri did not—his wife; but by always calling him "the famous American author," Antonio Vieri had something the famous American author did not—a full and proper name. Antonio Vieri would have explained this reasoning to the American if the American had asked. He didn't. He just stood there smiling at Antonio Vieri, rubbing his hands together as though he'd been cold and Antonio Vieri was a fire.

"Do you have any buddies?" the American said, placing his right hand on Antonio Vieri's shoulder.

"Buddies?"

"Pals, amigos, *friends*," the American said. "Someone to help you."

"I did, but then I told them to go away forever."

"Well, you're definitely going to need some help, and pronto," the American said. He removed his right hand from Antonio Vieri's shoulder and stuck it in Antonio Vieri's direction, and Antonio Vieri shook it. "Good deal," the American said. "My name is Brad."

BRAD WAS RIGHT: Antonio Vieri was going to need some help. This was in Florence, after all; it was the first week of July, and there wasn't an empty room in the city. The tourists were a hundred deep at Il Duomo. They were turning away people at the Uffizi. Even the lesser Medici houses were full to the point of suffocation. Competition between guided tours had become fierce. Just the day before, Brad told him, ten guided Germans had been trampled by twenty guided Swedes trying to get into an obscure Franciscan monastery whose monks were notable for nothing except their unusual methods of cheesemaking. There were too many sightseers, and all of them needed to see something, anything.

"You're going to be famous, man," Brad told Antonio Vieri. He was busy making the apartment even more pitiable than it had been. Brad picked up a few of Antonio Vieri's soiled clothes off the chair, ran them across the dusty floor, crumpled them up into loose balls, and then threw them against the front door, where they struck with soft, soiled thuds, then slid to the floor. The dirty clothes wads would be first thing someone would see, or not see and thus step on, when they walked through the door, the new doormat for the newly opened Pity Palace.

"I do not ever leave the apartment," Antonio Vieri said. "I cannot become famous if I don't leave my apartment."

"Yes, you can," Brad said. "I'm telling you."

"Are you warning me?" Antonio Vieri said. "My friends warned me, and that's why I told them to go away."

"You're one sad piece of work, aren't you?" Brad said, shaking his head appreciatively. "I'm not warning you at all. Just relax, OK?"

"If I'm going to be famous in my apartment," Antonio Vieri said, "maybe we should clean up a little." He felt nervous and a little giddy, as though he was about to go on a date—which he'd never done—or as though he was about to go out and find a wife and friends, which he had.

"Absofuckinglutely not," Brad said. "We want you to be as pitiable as possible. Let me take care of everything. Will you just let me take care of everything?"

"Are you—what is the expression?—telling me a playful but harmless lie?" by which Antonio Vieri meant, *Of course. Please take care of everything. That is exactly what I want you to do.* It was some sort of miracle, if you thought about it: Antonio Vieri had had friends to take care of him until they wouldn't stop warning him and he sent them away. And then just after he'd sent them away, Brad showed up, willing to take care of him but with no desire to warn him at all. It was as though all you had to do was *need* someone to take care of you, and then they would show up and do that. Was this the way the world could work? It seemed that it could, and that made Antonio Vieri happy, but only for a second. Because the problem with someone taking care of you is that there is always someone else you'd rather have take care of you. Once someone is taking care of you, you can't help but think of the someone who isn't.

"I miss my wife so much," Antonio Vieri said.

"That's the spirit," Brad said. "But speaking of your wife, I should probably know a few things about her before people show up."

"Of course," Antonio Vieri said. "What is the expression?— please start shooting me with your weapon."

Again, Brad shook his head, as though he couldn't believe his good fortune. "Right," he said. "Tell me something about her."

"She ate her *insalata mista* . . ."

"Yeah, yeah, and she read the best-selling novels," Brad said. "I know that already. That's only two things. What else did she do?"

"What else?" Antonio Vieri asked. Did there need to be something else? Were two things not enough? How many things did one need to do? How many things did the patriarch of the gangsters do? He brushed his cheeks with his fingers, and he told people that—what was the expression?—he'd concoct a deal whose terms they had no choice but to accept. How many things did you have to know about someone in order to love them, and to miss them once they were gone?

"Yeah, what else?" Brad said. "Tell me how you and your wife met."

"I found her," Antonio Vieri said. "I was sitting alone in this apartment, staring at the cracked plaster walls, and I said to myself, out loud, in the manner of the truly lonely, 'Antonio Vieri, if you do not find a wife, if you do not find friends, then you are going to end up in this apartment all alone for the rest of your life. You are going to end up as the saddest man in Florence. I am warning you.' And so I went out and found them."

"What do you mean, you '*found* them'?" Brad asked. He had that puzzled look on his face you get when you think you have one thing and then you find out that it's something else entirely. Antonio Vieri knew the look. It was the same look his wife had had when he had told her to leave him for the famous American author. "Do you mean you *met* them?"

"Do I?" Antonio Vieri said. He thought this might be, as with the vernacular in the best-selling novels, a problem with translation. "Maybe I do mean that. What is the difference?"

Just then, there was a knock on the door. Antonio Vieri stood up to answer it, but Brad motioned for him to sit down in the chair. Antonio Vieri did; Brad placed *The Final Patriarch of the Gangsters Once More* in Antonio Vieri's hands, then mussed Antonio Vieri's hair, which was sparse and considerably mussed already. On the table next to the chair, there was an opened jar of black olives, the label yellowed and corroded and nearly unreadable, one overly soaked and aged black olive swimming buddyless in the dingy brine. Next to the jar there was a two-year-old newspaper opened to a half-completed two-year-old crossword puzzle. On the floor, next to Antonio Vieri's chair, was a tower of the famous American's best-selling novels about Italian gangsters in New York, teetering toward the man who had read them too many times, and away from the window, away from the piazza, away from the man who had written them and who was now drinking wine in an outdoor café. All of these things—the books, the newspapers, even the olive—were originally meant to give Antonio Vieri comfort; but now, gathered and displayed as they were, they made him almost unbearably sad: there is nothing worse than seeing all the things you use to make yourself feel better gathered together in one place. Antonio Vieri felt terrible, but he could tell Brad felt good: Brad surveyed the scene, gave Antonio Vieri a satisfied nod, then opened the door.

"Is this the Pity Palace?"

Antonio Vieri couldn't see the speaker, but it was a woman's voice, an American, yet another one.

"Yes," Brad said. "Admission is ten euros."

"Each?"

"Each."

Antonio Vieri heard some grumbling, then zipper sounds. He leaned forward to get a glimpse of his first paying customers, and, in doing so, grazed the leaning tower of books with his elbow, and then the tower was no more: the books fell with that raspy paperback sound, some of them falling on the floor,

but most of them on Antonio Vieri. He yelped and brushed
the books off of him, as if they were ashes from the cigarettes
he didn't smoke. When he looked up, he saw his first paying
customers, gaping at him.

There were two of them, a man and a woman. It was clear
that both of them could really—what was the expression?—
fasten a sack over their faces out of which they would eat like
hungry animals. Their round faces glistened with sweat and
the remnants of their midmorning gelati. The man wore a cap
pulled way down over his forehead, almost to the eyebrows;
the cap was sky blue, and was adorned with a white cross, or
rather several white crosses, layered on top of one another,
each one slightly bigger then the next, which gave Antonio
Vieri the impression that the cross might at any minute burst
right out of the sky-blue cap and into the unsuspecting secular
world. The woman had the sort of severely blunt haircut that
signifies either piety or retardation; she was wearing a shiny
green windbreaker on which the name Donna was written in
cursive over the right breast. Both the man and Donna wore
the overlarge belts that Antonio Vieri knew were called "fanny
packs"; he also knew what a "fanny" was and could not understand why, then, the belts were worn around the stomach
and not the fanny. All he knew for sure was that they were
ridiculous. Perhaps if the famous American author had worn a
fanny pack, Antonio Vieri's wife would not have left Antonio
Vieri. But Antonio Vieri guessed that he didn't, and she had.

Donna approached Antonio Vieri warily, hesitantly, as if

he were a hungry lion and she, the woman, had forgotten to bring the meat. The man hung back, head down, as though ashamed. Donna was holding in her meaty hands the flyer that Antonio Vieri's friends had made and disseminated; she consulted it quickly, and then looked back at Antonio Vieri.

"You're Antonio Vieri?"

"It is I." He glanced at Brad, and Brad nodded. They'd rehearsed. Antonio Vieri cleared his throat and said: "My wife left me for the famous American author who wrote those bestselling novels about Italian gangsters in New York. I miss her so much. I even miss the way she ate her *insalata mista*. She ate her *insalata mista* so delicately, one leaf at a time, like an angel. Now she is gone, and I am the saddest man in Florence. This is my home. This is the Pity Palace." At this, Antonio Vieri made a sweeping gesture with his right arm, as though inviting Donna to see how pitiable his palace was. But Donna didn't notice: she'd been looking at the flyer, reading along from the text of Antonio Vieri's speech. After a few seconds of silence, it must have been clear to Donna that he had nothing more to say: she raised her head, looked at him, then at Brad, and said, "That's it? That's not so bad. I don't feel sorry for you much at all." Donna's lips, her cheeks, her whole face, quivered with disappointment. If the gelato on her chin, her upper lip, and her cheeks was makeup, then the disappointment was something that couldn't be covered. Antonio Vieri felt sorry for her; it was the first time he'd felt sorry for anyone else. It was like finding money in your pocket, money you'd never had, never lost, money you didn't know you'd ever wanted. "You don't seem so sad."

"I don't?"

"He does," Brad said. Antonio Vieri could hear the yelp of panic in his voice, could see that Brad hadn't pocketed the twenty euros, as though he wasn't sure they truly belonged to him yet.

"He doesn't," Donna said, then sighed and cocked her head in the direction of her husband. "But go ahead, Steve. We're here. You might as well go ahead show him your mole."

Steve took two steps forward, pulled off his hat, and showed Antonio Vieri his mole. It was on his forehead, just above the hairless space between his eyebrows, which was why Steve had worn his hat so low. The mole was the size of an eye, was black, except where it was purple, and had topography: little mountains crusted with something white, shallow valleys of the deepest, most malignant purple. In one of the valleys there seemed to be a thin stream of pus. The mole looked angry, angrier even than the littlest Italian gangsters with the most to prove in the famous American author's best-selling novels, so angry that it throbbed. Antonio Vieri could see hairs growing out or through the mole, wiggling frantically, as though trying to escape. The hat had put a crease in the mole, making the southern tip look like it had seceded from the rest of the sovereign mole.

"Ouch," said Brad.

Steve didn't say anything, as though he were resigned to let his mole and his Donna do all his talking for him. He put his hat back on and receded again into the apartment's shadows.

"I know," Donna said. "We've prayed. We've prayed and prayed for the Lord to rid Steve of his mole. We've even prayed for the Lord to make it cancer. 'Please, Jesus, make it cancer.' That was our exact prayer. The insurance won't pay for getting rid of it unless it's cancer. But it's not cancer. Jesus in his mystery and wisdom won't make it cancer, not even precancer. I don't know why. All I know is that it's ugly. I'm sorry, Steve, but it is: I can see it even through the hat; I can see it even though you're way over there in the corner. Even with my eyes closed, I can see it. Watch. Here I am, closing my eyes, and I can still see it. There it is, Jesus, the way you made it. You died for our sins, and then You made Steve's hideous mole."

"Ouch," Brad said again.

Donna opened her eyes and nodded. "It's come between us."

Antonio Vieri could see how that could happen. It happened in the best-selling novels all the time: someone murdered his brother, and the murder came between the murderer and his other brother; someone murdered his father, and the murder came between the murderer and his mother; someone lied to his wife about all the murdering, and the lying and murdering came between the lying murderer and his wife. It seemed, to Antonio Vieri, that if Donna's Jesus existed, then He made two people and not one only so that someone or something would then come between them. The best-selling novels *and* their famous American author had come between

Antonio Vieri and his wife, and now it was clear that Donna and Steve and Steve's mole were about to come between Brad and Antonio Vieri, too. Antonio Vieri could see the blank, horrified look on Brad's face. Earlier, Brad had confided that before he'd met Antonio Vieri, nothing had ever worked out for him, not in love, not in anything. "My last job was working for a dry cleaner," he'd told Antonio Vieri. "But then I got fired for not keeping the dry cleaning dry enough. My boss said he'd never seen anything like it. Do you understand what I'm telling you?" Antonio Vieri had: he understood how easily pity became self-pity, understood that if Antonio Vieri and his Pity Palace became just one more thing that didn't work out for Brad, Brad would leave him, and he would be all alone again.

"The story I've told you," Antonio Vieri said quietly, as though telling them a secret, "that is not the whole story." Once he'd said that, Antonio Vieri could feel the difference in the room. It was like the wind had picked up, blown the despair out of the room, and replaced it, not with something else, but with the *hope* that it would be something else, something better. It was like that moment in one of the best-selling novels, after the middle-brother gangster has confessed to betraying the younger-brother gangster, but before he knows whether the younger-brother gangster will forgive him or murder him. Donna and Brad leaned toward Antonio Vieri expectantly; even Steve seemed to move out of the shadows a little bit. "My wife liked to eat *insalata mista*—that much has been told. And I would just sit around and watch her eat: she was that beautiful. That's all she did; that's all I wanted her to do. I thought I never would get tired of it."

"But then you did," Donna said, nodding, as if she were hearing an old story, one of her favorites. "Jesus gave you everything you wanted, and then Satan made you want more."

It was true. Antonio Vieri remembered the moment too clearly. He and his wife were sitting at the kitchen table; he was watching her eat her *insalata mista* delicately, one leaf at a time, like an *angel*, just like she had the day before, and the day before that, and all Antonio Vieri could think of was what it would be like to sit there and watch his wife eat her *insalata mista* like this for eternity, and so he said, out of the blue, "Maybe you'd like something to read," and gave her one of the famous American author's best-selling novels about Italian gangsters in New York.

"You mean one of these?" Donna asked, as if she had not really noticed the books scattered around before that moment. She picked up one of the books—*The Proper Italian Word for Death*—and held it so anxiously, so uncertainly, Antonio Vieri wondered whether she'd ever even held a book before. "Where did all these books come from, anyway?"

"They—what is the expression?—tumbled off of a moving construction vehicle." In truth, Antonio Vieri didn't remember where they'd come from. Perhaps the previous tenants had left them, although Antonio Vieri didn't remember anyone living in the apartment before him, nor did he remember living in another apartment but this one. Perhaps his friends had brought him the books, although Antonio Vieri didn't remember his friends bringing him anything but food. But what did it matter? Where does anyone get anything? You are lonely, and so you go find a wife to make you less so. You want the wife who makes you feel less lonely to read something to supplement her delicate, angelic eating of her *insalata mista*, and so you give her a book. The world is not so mysterious. Antonio Vieri's wife had said, "Yes, I'd love something to read," and luckily, Antonio Vieri had one of the best-selling novels to give her, no matter where it'd come from.

"Did she like it?" Donna asked. She looked dubiously at the book in her hands, as though wondering how anyone could like such a thing.

"She *loved* it," Antonio Vieri said. He could hear the jealousy in his voice, could feel it in the back of his throat. "She loved *all* of them. She loved them so much that's all she did; she barely even ate her *insalata mista* anymore, and when she did, she'd eat big fistfuls of it so that she could get back to the novels. So one day . . ." And then Antonio Vieri stopped. He had the urge to apologize—not to anyone in the room, but to his wife. He wanted to crawl deep into her ear and whisper, *I'm sorry, I love you, I'm sorry, I love you*, until that was the only thing she could hear, until she knew that it was true.

"Tell us, Antonio Vieri," Donna said. Steve had emerged from the shadows and was standing next to his wife; they were holding hands. "Jesus wants you tell us so we can feel better about Steve's hideous mole."

Antonio Vieri cleared his throat once, twice, thrice, closed his eyes, and then said, "And so one day I told her that it seemed like she loved the best-selling novels more than she loved me. I told her that if she loved the best-selling novels so much, then why didn't she leave me for the man who wrote them?"

"And then she did. You poor guy," Donna said, and Antonio Vieri nodded. "She actually left you for the famous American author." She turned to Steve, her face shining and holy. "Take your hat off, Steve. Jesus made your hideous mole, but He also gave us this poor man and his story."

But Steve didn't take off his hat. He moved closer to Antonio Vieri, squinting, as though trying to see him more clearly. Antonio Vieri was slumped in his chair. He'd never told the whole story to anyone before, not even his friends before he'd sent them away. Now that he'd told it to Steve and Donna, he wished he hadn't: he felt dead, like everything to know about him was known, and none of it was good. Antonio Vieri wondered if this was what the middle-gangster brother had felt after confessing to his younger-gangster brother, and wondered, already feeling dead, if he minded so terribly much when his younger-gangster brother then had him killed. "Let me get this straight," Steve said. "Your wife kept reading these books—"

"The best-selling novels about Italian gangsters in New York," Antonio Vieri said. "Yes, she did."

"And one day you told her that she should leave you for the famous American author—"

"And so she did that," Antonio Vieri said.

"And the famous American author was in Florence," Steve said. "He just happened to be in Florence, and your wife just happened to know he was in Florence."

"Obviously," Antonio Vieri said. "Otherwise, how would she have left me for him?" Antonio Vieri suddenly was tired of answering Steve's stupid questions with their obvious answers. He wished Steve would let Donna and his mole do the talking for him again. He wished Steve and his mole would retreat to the shadows of the apartment, wished Steve and his wife would leave the apartment, wished they would go away forever just like Antonio Vieri's friends had.

"And that's her?" Steve said, pointing to the two caricatures on the wall.

"I drew those myself," Antonio Vieri said. "Crudely, but with all my heart."

"Why does he *talk* that way?" Steve asked Brad. Brad shrugged and pretended to look at something interesting on the floor, and so Steve asked Antonio Vieri, "Why do you *talk* that way?"

"What way?"

"Why do you only say a few things, and why do you say those few things the same way every time you say them?" Steve said. "'The famous American author,' the 'best-selling novels,' 'the *insalata mista*.' You sound fake."

"I don't," Antonio Vieri said.

"You do," Steve said. "Maybe that's why your wife left you for the famous American author."

"She left me for the famous American author because I told her to," Antonio Vieri said, but Steve didn't seem to be listening. He was over by the caricatures, looking at them, scrutinizing them.

"These are so bad she could be any woman," Steve said. "Or no woman at all. Don't you have any *photos* of your wife?"

"I do not have a camera," Antonio Vieri said. Steve made a scoffing noise at this. But it was the truth. Antonio Vieri didn't have a camera. Was it so strange that he didn't have a camera? "After all, if I'd had a camera, I wouldn't have had to draw the crude caricatures."

"This is unbelievable," Steve said to his wife, who was staring at him, gape-mouthed, as though he was an entirely different Steve. It was like the moment when the youngest-brother gangster becomes the patriarch, and all the other gangsters stare at him, gape-mouthed, as though he were an entirely different younger brother. "This is unbelievable," he said to Brad. "We're really supposed to believe that his wife left him—"

"It's true," Antonio Vieri said. "The famous American author is right outside in the piazza, drinking wine in the café."

"He is?" Brad said, and looked with surprise in the direction of the window, as if realizing for the first time that the apartment had one. He walked to the window and looked out. "Hey, there *is* someone out there."

"Oh, come on," Steve said, walking over to the window to see for himself.

"I know," Antonio Vieri said. "Out of all the outdoor cafés in all the piazzas in all of Florence, the famous American author has to drink red wine in this one, and he's been out there every day since my wife left me for him."

"You're trying to tell me that that guy is Mario Puzo," Steve began, but Antonio Vieri shrieked, "You are not allowed to refer to him by that name in this apartment!" and then ran into his bedroom; he could hear Brad say to Steve and his wife, "In the Pity Palace you may call him 'the famous American author' or you may call him nothing at all. I forgot to mention that." And then Antonio Vieri slammed the bedroom door behind him and dove into his bed, the bed he'd not slept in since his wife had left him, his head jammed under his pillow. After a few minutes, he could hear the door creak open, could hear footsteps coming closer, could feel someone's hand on his shoulder.

"Did they go away?" Antonio Vieri asked, his head still under the pillow.

"Yup," Brad said.

"Did they go away forever?"

"Probably," Brad said. "But there are going to be others. You were a big hit, bud. Steve and his wife said they were going to tell everyone. You should have seen them. They were two totally different animals by the time you were done with them. She even kissed his mole on their way out." Antonio Vieri groaned, and Brad said, "I know, it was grim," and Antonio Vieri groaned again, and Brad said, "Are you OK?"

"No," Antonio Vieri said, because he wasn't: because the more he'd talked about his wife, his friends, the *insalata mista*, the famous American author and his best-selling novels, *everything*, the less real they'd seemed. Earlier, he'd wanted to crawl into his wife's ear so that she wouldn't hear anything except how much he loved her, how sorry he was; now he wanted her to crawl into his mouth until there was no room in there for anything else, no room even for words, so that he wouldn't be able to say anything else about her, about them, about anything. Because Antonio Vieri knew now that the more you talked about something, the less real it seemed. *This* was why he talked the way he talked; this was why the Italian gangsters in New York talked the way *they* talked, too, using only their expressions. They knew what Antonio Vieri knew: that in order to keep the things that mattered real, you had to say only a few things, and the few things you said had to be the same every time you said them.

"What can I do?" Brad asked him.

"Tell everyone to go away forever."

"I've never had anything work out for me before now," Brad said, and just then, there was a knock on the door. Antonio Vieri could hear it through his pillow. "I was the first person ever who couldn't even keep the dry cleaning *dry* enough. I can't tell them to go away."

"Fine," Antonio Vieri said, sighing. "I will tell them that my wife ate *insalata mista* like an angel and that she left me for the famous American author, and that is all."

AND THAT WAS all Antonio Vieri told them, the Americans who filled his apartment day after day. Because the only people who entered the Pity Palace were Americans. Antonio Vieri was sure this was meaningful, although he couldn't say, with any certainty, what it might mean. Perhaps it meant that only Americans felt better about themselves by seeing the misery of others. Perhaps it meant that only Americans needed to feel better about themselves. Or perhaps it meant that only American read flyers handed to them in piazzas by strange old coots. In any case, they filled his apartment, decked out in their fanny packs, standing over his bed, waiting for him to say something.

"I am Antonio Vieri. My wife left me for the famous American author who wrote those best-selling novels about Italian gangsters in New York," he told them. "I miss her so much. I even miss the way she ate her *insalata mista*. She ate her *insalata mista* so delicately, one leaf at a time. She ate her *insalata mista* like an *angel*. Now go away."

"For how long?" they asked.

"Forever," Antonio Vieri said.

"OK, folks," Brad said, ushering them out of the bedroom. "I'd be happy to answer any of your questions . . ." And then Antonio Vieri stuck his head under the pillow and could hear no more.

This went on for days, or maybe months. Years? Antonio

Vieri had no idea. Every day was like the one before. Every day, he awoke to find people staring at him, his caricatures, his books, his filthy apartment; every day, he said what he would say, and then told his visitors to go away forever, which they did, to the next room, where Brad answered their questions. And Antonio Vieri knew what their questions were, too, knew they wanted to know what Steve had wanted to know—namely, was Antonio Vieri serious? Can't he talk about anything except this *insalata mista*? Can someone really miss the way someone else eats *salad*? Does he really believe that his wife left him for the famous American author? Does he really believe he might get her back by reading the famous American author's best-selling novels? That guy, way across the piazza: Does he really believe *that* guy is the famous American author? Does he really believe that he even had a wife in the first place? And what's the deal with these caricatures, anyway? And why does being here, in this place, make me feel so good about myself? Is there a sadder man in all of Florence? Is there a sadder man *anywhere*? Antonio Vieri knew they were asking Brad these questions. He asked them of himself, and each time he asked himself, *Is she real? Did I just make her up so I wouldn't be alone?* he felt so sad, so lonely, the way he'd felt when he *knew* his wife was real, when he *knew* she'd left him for the famous American author. Could you feel this sad, this lonely, about someone who wasn't real, someone who was just in your head? You couldn't, could you?

"She is a real person," Antonio Vieri said to Brad one day.

Brad was sitting on the edge of Antonio Vieri's bed, divvying up the money—one euro for Antonio Vieri, one euro for Brad, etc. There was so much money that it didn't seem as though Brad would ever be able to divvy it all up in one sitting. But the money, and the ability to make it, didn't seem to make Brad happy anymore; as he counted the money, he looked washed-out, weary, resigned. Antonio Vieri said, "I could not feel this sad, this lonely, about someone who wasn't real. You believe that she is a real person, don't you?"

"I'd like to," Brad said. "But every day these people ask their questions and I can't answer them. Today, someone asked me what your wife's name was. I couldn't tell them. I told them you referred to her only as 'my wife.'"

"That's true," Antonio Vieri said.

"I felt like an idiot," Brad said. "Does your wife even have a name?"

"She does," Antonio Vieri said. "It is Connie."

"Dude," Brad said. "Come on. That's the name of the sister in the best-selling novels."

"I know," Antonio Vieri said. "My wife and I laughed over that coincidence many a time before she left me for the famous American author."

Brad shook his head; he took his half of the euros and pushed them across the bed toward Antonio Vieri. "It's not worth it anymore," Brad said. "You make me too sad."

"Are you saying she's not a real person?" Antonio Vieri said. "Are you saying I made her up? Did I make up this?" And here Antonio Vieri picked up a fistful of cash and threw it at Brad. Brad stood up and started walking away; Antonio Vieri picked up a flyer, announcing the opening of the Pity Palace, and asked, "Did I make this up, too? Did I make up the old coots who gave it to you? Did I make up the best-selling novels? Did I make up the man sitting at the far edge of the piazza? Did I make up these?" Antonio Vieri asked, and pointed to the tears pouring down his checks, his chin: because his wife had left him, and he had sent his friends away, and now Brad was going away, too—whether Antonio Vieri told him to go away, or asked him to stay, Antonio Vieri knew that Brad was going—and once that happened, he would be all alone, again, and maybe forever. "Did I make up *you*?" Antonio Vieri asked him.

"You make me too sad," Brad said. "It doesn't matter to me anymore." And then he left the room; Antonio Vieri could hear footsteps, could hear the apartment door creak open, slam shut, and then nothing.

Antonio Vieri wondered if maybe Brad was right. After all, if losing your wife made you feel the same as suspecting your wife wasn't real, and had never been a real person for you to lose, then what did it matter? What did it matter if a person was real, or if you just made them up, if either way you felt lonely once they were gone? Was loneliness the only real thing in this world? If it was, then what did it matter if there was a Brad or if there wasn't a Brad? Was Brad himself real outside of Antonio Vieri's loneliness? Was anyone? Was there anyone who could tell you what was real or not in this world? And if so, where, oh where, if you were Antonio Vieri, could you find this person, these people? How could you make them find you?

There was a knock on the apartment door. Antonio Vieri put the pillow over his head and waited for the knocking to stop, waited for whoever was knocking to realize that the Pity Palace was closed, and to go away. After a few minutes, the knocking seemed to stop. Antonio Vieri removed the pillow again and looked up, and there, at the foot of his bed, was a group of men.

The group seemed to be divided into two factions. One faction had salt-and-pepper beards and wore corduroy jackets; the other faction had slicked-back hair and wore gold necklaces and black leather jackets. The men in corduroy each held a copy of one of the famous American author's best-selling novels—except unlike Antonio Vieri's beat-up paperbacks, their books were hardcover and preserved in slick plastic sleeves. The men in black leather didn't have books; instead, they stood with their feet far apart, cracking their knuckles. Antonio Vieri suddenly felt very nervous, as though these men were a government licensing agency and Antonio Vieri didn't have the proper government license.

"Who are you?" Antonio Vieri asked.

"We're from the Mario Puzo Society," said one of the men in corduroy.

This made Antonio Vieri sit up in bed, made him forget that, in the Pity Palace, one was supposed to call him "the famous American author" or nothing at all. "He has his own society?"

"He does," said another one of the men in corduroy. You could see the grooves in his beard from where he'd stroked it thoughtfully. "We are it."

"What does his society do?" Antonio Vieri asked. "Do you read the books and then talk about them, how much you love them? Do you say the expressions to each other?"

"We hold meetings, mostly," said another man in corduroy. The men in black leather hadn't spoken; like Steve with his mole and his Donna, they seemed content to let their knuckles and their corduroyed colleagues speak for them. "We were holding our annual meeting in Palermo, and then we heard there was someone in Florence claiming that his wife had left him for Mario Puzo."

At that, the men in black leather drew themselves up to their full height, as though to ward off a threat. "Who are *they*?" Antonio Vieri whispered, nodding in the direction of the knuckle crackers.

The men in corduroy didn't answer; instead, they squinted skeptically at Antonio Vieri. "Are you even Italian?" one of them asked, and then, to the other men in corduroy, "Is this guy even Italian?"

The other men in corduroy shook their heads in dismay.

"Doesn't look Italian at all." "Never seen anyone look *less* like a goombah in my life." "Is it possible that he's *Swiss*?" "Does anyone know what a *Swiss* looks like?"

"Of course I'm Italian," Antonio Vieri said. He was out of bed now, on his feet for the first time in he didn't know how long. He felt weak, too. When was the last time he'd stood? When was the last time he'd eaten? He remembered Brad offering him some of the healthy candy bars and Antonio Vieri, full of self-pity, refusing to eat them. "How do you know so much about what an Italian looks like?"

"That's why we keep these guys around," the first man in corduroy said, hooking his thumb at the men in black leather. "To remind us. But that is not the point. The point is that we heard that an Antonio Vieri of Florence was walking around, saying that Mario Puzo had stolen his wife. And one of the duties of the Mario Puzo Society is to defend his legacy."

"What is his legacy?"

"Whatever we say it is," the first man in corduroy said.

"Well, it's true," Antonio Vieri said. "My wife left me for your famous American author."

"It is not true," the first man in corduroy said.

"How do you know?"

"Because he's dead," the first man in corduroy said. "He died seven years, four months, and twenty-eight days ago."

"If he's so dead," Antonio Vieri said, "then why is he sitting at the outdoor café in the piazza, drinking red wine?" He could hear the whine in his voice, the desperation, and although he had every right to feel desperate, he had no right to whine. After all, this was what Antonio Vieri had asked for: he'd asked for someone who knew what was real to find him, and he had gotten what he'd asked for. Except he didn't want it anymore: he did not want to know.

"What café?" The men in corduroy suddenly looked nervous: they tugged at their jackets, furiously stroked their beards, then combed their hair with their fingers. The men in leather, seeing their colleagues' nervousness, doubled their knuckle-cracking in an attempt, Antonio Vieri guessed, to become even more Italian. Antonio Vieri swore that their skin turned swarthier, their hair greasier, their gold necklaces thicker, the Italian horns on the necklaces more hornlike. "What piazza?"

"The one right outside," Antonio Vieri said, and pointed at the window.

With that, the men in corduroy rushed to the window. Antonio Vieri couldn't see them—the men in black leather placed themselves between their fellow society members and Antonio Vieri—but he could hear them, all talking at once: "Jesus, is that him?" "It can't be him; he never once drank red wine. You know that." "Plus, he's dead." "Well, it *looks* like him." "It doesn't." "It does." "It's like a *caricature* of him." "It could be anyone. Or no one." "Or him." "If only he weren't on the far edge of the piazza." "Get your binoculars, man." "Who is that he's sitting with?" "I think it's a woman." I *know* it's a woman. I don't need any effing *binoculars* to tell me it's a *woman*." "Wait a minute. Is that the woman in this guy's caricatures." "Impossible to tell, they're so crudely drawn." "It *might* be her." "Might, might, might." "She's eating salad in the pictures. But she's not eating salad down there." "What is that? Is she eating a *pancake* or something?" "She's not eating a pancake. Where do you get a pancake in Florence?" "All I know is that whatever she's eating, they're round, and there is a big stack of them." "You can tell that from up here?" "Jesus, why don't we just go down there and see if it's him." "*You* go down there; I'm staying here, in this guy's apartment, with his books and his olive." "Well, *someone* sure as hell better go." "Why don't we send our Italian brothers in black leather?" But the men in black leather weren't going anywhere: by this point they'd closed their eyes, as though trying to wish themselves into another apartment, with another group of men, who were wearing another sort of jacket, who were looking out the window at another sort of author, who wrote another sort of novel. "I've got an idea," one of the men in corduroy said. "Why don't we just wait for someone to come up here and tell us if it's really him or not?" "Wait, what was that sound?" another one asked. "Was that a knock on the door?"

It wasn't a knock on the door: it was the sound of Antonio Vieri closing the apartment door behind him. He had trouble handling the stairs: he was four stories up, after all, and hadn't walked or eaten in who knows how long. But that was all right, because at the bottom of the stairs, at the far edge of the piazza, there was a woman eating something—pancakes maybe, whatever those were, and she had a big stack of them—

and whoever it was—wife, or not wife; real or not real—maybe she would share them. Maybe once they were done eating, she would leave the famous American author for him, and maybe, if she wasn't his wife, she would let him call her his wife, and maybe if she wasn't real, she would let him call her real, and maybe she would take him away to another sort of apartment, in another sort of city, where maybe Antonio Vieri would say more than just a few things, or maybe he would say the same few things but would say them differently every time he said them, or maybe he would learn from his mistakes and let his wife talk for a change and then mimic her expressions, and maybe he would let his wife eat whatever sort of food she wanted and read whatever sort of novel by whatever sort of author and be content to know however many things about her that she wanted him to know, and maybe there would never be a reason for someone to knock on their door and so never a reason for them to answer it, and maybe Antonio Vieri wouldn't ever need to feel sorry for himself again, and maybe this time it would work out for him and his wife and they would be happy, truly and finally happy, to have found each other again, just when they needed each other the most, just like in a book.

# Acknowledgments

Thanks to:

The editors of the magazines and anthologies where these stories first appeared: William Pierce, Ben George, Emily Smith, Anna Lena Phillips Bell, Hannah Tinti, Speer Morgan, Sy Safransky, Carol Ann Fitzgerald, Bill Henderson, Ted Genoways, Carolyn Kuebler, Merrill Feitell, and Jodee Stanley.

These writers for their support and advice during the time I was writing these stories: Nicola Mason, Leah Stewart, Kevin Moffett, Corinna Vallianatos, Jess Anthony, Jason Ockert, Jeff Parker, Erica Dawson, Pete Coviello, Mike Paterniti, Sara Corbett, Lewis Robinson, Justin Tussing, Rick Russo, and Jennifer Brice.

My friends, colleagues, and students at Cincinnati, Bowdoin, Tampa, and Colgate.

My agent, Elizabeth Sheinkman, and my editor, Chuck Adams.

My family: Lane, Quinn, and Ambrose.